PUSH

CW01391475

THE
PODOLIAN
NIGHTS

NACHMAN OF BRATSLAV (1772–1810) was born into a family of important figures in Hasidism in Międzybóż in the Polish–Lithuanian Commonwealth, now Medzhybizh in Ukraine. After initially refusing to carry on the family's tradition of Jewish spiritual leadership, Nachman assumed leadership in Hasidism after a journey to Israel in 1798–99. After moving to the town of Bratslav in 1802, he met Nathan Sternhartz, who began recording all of Nachman's lessons and who would go on to transcribe the stories in this collection.

ROBERT ADLER PECKERAR is a translator and cultural historian. He is the Executive Director of Yiddishkayt, the West Coast's premier Yiddish cultural organization, and the CEO of the Topa Institute, an intercultural arts and education center based in the Ojai Valley, California.

JORDAN FINKIN is the rare book and manuscript librarian at Hebrew Union College in Cincinnati. A scholar of modern Yiddish literature, he is also a literary translator from Yiddish, French, and German.

ADAM KIRSCH is the author of several books of poetry and criticism. A 2016 Guggenheim Fellow, Kirsch is an editor at the *Wall Street Journal*'s Weekend Review section and has written for publications including the *New Yorker* and *Tablet*. He lives in New York.

THE
PODOLIAN
NIGHTS
ESSENTIAL TALES

NACHMAN
OF
BRATSLAV

TRANSLATED FROM THE YIDDISH
BY ROBERT ADLER PECKERAR
AND JORDAN FINKIN

WITH AN INTRODUCTION
BY ADAM KIRSCH

PUSHKIN PRESS CLASSICS

Pushkin Press
Somerset House, Strand
London WC2R 1LA

Nachman's tales were first published posthumously by
Nathan Sternhartz as *Sipurey Mayses* in 1815

First published by Pushkin Press in 2025

ISBN 13: 978-1-80533-123-0

Designed and typeset by Tetragon, London
Printed and bound in the United Kingdom by Clays Ltd, Elcograf S.p.A.

EU RP (for authorities only): eucomply OÜ, Pärnu mnt. 139b-14, 11317,
Tallinn, Estonia, hello@eucompliancepartner.com, +3375769024I

www.pushkinpress.com

1 3 5 7 9 8 6 4 2

Pushkin Press is committed to a sustainable future for our
business, our readers and our planet. This book is made from
paper from forests that support responsible forestry.

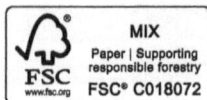

MIX
Paper | Supporting
responsible forestry
FSC
www.fsc.org
FSC® C018072

Contents

Introduction

In the twentieth century, Hasidic tales became known to the wider world as a treasure of folk literature. For the first Jews who told and retold them, however, in the Eastern European borderlands of the mid-eighteenth century, they were more than literature; they were themselves religious acts. Repeating a story about the Baal Shem Tov, the wonder-working rabbi who was the founder of Hasidism, was a way of testifying to his holiness and spreading the good news of his teachings. These stories circulated orally for decades after he died, and were collected in print for the first time in 1815 in a volume titled 'In Praise of the Baal Shem Tov'.

Around the same time, a very different kind of Hasidic tale made its appearance in print: the 'Fabulous Tales', but translated into English simply as *Tales*, of Rabbi Nachman of Bratslav. Nachman was Hasidic royalty: his mother was the granddaughter of the Baal Shem Tov, and his uncle Baruch was an important rabbi in his own right. From the moment he was born, in 1772, Nachman carried as heavy a burden of expectation as any prince. Nothing could be more natural than that such a man would grow up to be a tzaddik, a 'righteous man' and Hasidic leader.

Yet the *Tales* of Rabbi Nachman are like nothing else in Hasidic literature. These are not tales about Nachman's holiness and miracle-working powers, passed down by his followers. Rather, they are stories invented by Nachman himself, first delivered orally to gatherings of his followers. Unlike the usual Hasidic tale, with its pious, didactic message, Nachman's stories are full of paradoxes and esoteric symbolism. The more deeply they are studied, the more enigmatic they become. For this reason, they have often struck readers as distinctively modern, akin to the legends of Hans Christian Andersen or the dark parables of Franz Kafka. To read Nachman's tales is to enter a world of elusive meanings, where the only thing certain is that the world as we know it is deeply broken.

Outwardly, Nachman's stories often resemble fairy tales. They are populated by princesses and kings and talking animals, and they feature babies switched at birth and heroes who go on quests. Scholars have found that they employ themes and plots common to folktales around the world, some of which Nachman must have absorbed from the surrounding non-Jewish cultures of Eastern Europe. Indeed, it is notable that the characters in these stories are seldom Jews, and the world they live in is not the world Nachman himself knew, but the wide world of royal courts and remote desert islands. His first listeners must have been startled by the way their holy tzaddik moved so easily in this imaginative realm. Perhaps that is why Nachman ironically deprecated his own stories: 'What can people find to complain about? After all, they are nice stories to tell,' he is quoted as saying in the introduction to the first edition of the *Tales*.

If Nachman's stories were controversial, that only made them a faithful reflection of their author. He was never one of the more popular Hasidic rabbis; his followers were a self-selected elite, willing to undergo rigorous disciplines. They were so dedicated to Nachman that after he died of tuberculosis in 1810, they did not select a relative or follower to replace him, as was standard in Hasidic courts. Rather, to this day, the Bratslaver Hasidim continue to see Nachman as their leader, for which reason they have been given the grim name of 'dead Hasidim'. Every year on Rosh Hashana, thousands of Bratslavers and other admirers of Nachman congregate in Uman, the Ukrainian city where he died, to celebrate his memory and worship at his grave.

The gaiety and simplicity reflected in the stories about the Baal Shem Tov are nowhere to be found in the anecdotes recorded about Nachman's life. 'No act in the service of God came easily to him; everything came only as a result of great and oft-repeated struggle,' wrote his follower Rabbi Nathan Sternhartz. Even as a child, 'he would often speak to God in heartfelt supplications and pleas… but nevertheless he felt he wasn't being noticed or heard at all. On the contrary, it seemed to him that he was being pushed away from the service of God in all kinds of ways, as though he were utterly unwanted.'

In response, Nachman turned towards the kind of self-tormenting asceticism that Hasidism usually preached against. As a child, he decided that he must overcome his pleasure in eating and began to swallow food in large pieces without chewing, so as not to taste it. As a teenager, he would fast from Sabbath to Sabbath and roll naked in the snow in winter. Rabbi Nathan compares Nachman's repeated assaults on his own body—above all, on his sexual urges—to military conquests: 'being a powerful warrior… he succeeded in overcoming his passions.' Haunted by the sense that he was unworthy to inherit his great-grandfather's mantle, Nachman created a religious style that was the opposite of the Baal Shem Tov's: not a simple celebration of God, but a kind of existential striving for Him.

The course of Nachman's adult life was correspondingly stormy. At the age of twenty-six, in 1798, he decided to undertake a pilgrimage to the Land of Israel. This was not an uncommon aspiration for Hasidic rabbis—his own grandfather had settled permanently in the Galilee—but Nachman made his trip at an especially dangerous moment, just as Napoleon's armies were embarking on their campaign in Egypt and Palestine. For Nachman, this was not an obstacle but an attraction: 'Know that I want to place myself in danger, even great and terrible danger,' he is supposed to have said. Indeed, just hours after he stepped off the boat in Haifa he announced that he wanted to return home, as if the ordeal of the journey had been the whole point. Only with difficulty was he persuaded to remain in the Holy Land for several months, visiting sacred sites and the small but growing Hasidic communities. On his return journey, Nachman ran into still more trouble: he sailed in a Turkish warship that was attacked by the French, narrowly avoided shipwreck, and had to be redeemed from captivity by the Jewish community of Rhodes.

Once he returned to Eastern Europe in 1799, Nachman settled in the town of Bratslav, where his followers began to preach that he was either the Messiah himself or else the key to his arrival. But the death of Nachman's only son, in 1806, seems to have put an end to his messianic ambitions. It was in the summer of that year, at a time of personal and religious crisis, that he began to tell his stories, usually during the gatherings of his followers that took place on Jewish holidays.

'When the Rebbe began telling stories,' according to Rabbi Nathan's introduction to the first edition of the *Tales*, 'he said "I am now beginning to tell stories." His intent was as if to say, "[I must tell stories] because my lessons and conversations are not having any effect in bringing you back to God."' Nachman believed in the redemptive function of storytelling: 'The world says that fabulous tales may put you to sleep, but I say that tales can wake people up,' he said. He went so far as to teach that even Gentile folktales contained the seeds of religious truth, though in distorted and confused form: 'Many hidden meanings and lofty concepts are contained in the stories that the world tells. These stories, however, are deficient; they contain many omissions. They are also confused, and people do not tell them in the right order.'

The clear implication is that Nachman's own stories are going to rectify this confusion, to tell the world's tales as they are meant to be told. And so it is appropriate that rectification—in Hebrew, *tikkun*—is the main theme of his tales. The phrase *tikkun olam*, 'repair of the world', is often used by Jews today to refer to social justice activism, but in Kabbalah, the tradition of Jewish mysticism, it has a very different meaning. In the sixteenth century, the great Kabbalist Isaac Luria elaborated the idea that divine 'sparks' left over from the Creation are hidden in our world, buried and obstructed by 'shells'. The task of the Jew is to liberate these sparks and return them to God, thus hastening the advent of the

Messiah. According to this activist mysticism, prayers and good deeds could literally repair the world.

For Nachman, telling tales served this redemptive purpose: the right story told in the right way could bring a person back to God. But it was necessary for the storyteller to proceed carefully, adapting his spiritual truths to the capacity of his audience. A blind man who has just been healed, Nachman once explained, must be protected from bright lights; even so, a person in a state of spiritual convalescence should not be exposed to the full glare of truth. A story is a therapeutic device, allowing the listener to uncover its meaning at his own pace.

The first edition of Nachman's *Tales* included thirteen stories (later editions added others, of more dubious authenticity). The simplest can barely be said to hide their spiritual message at all. Take 'Of a Rabbi and his Only Son', one of the shortest tales, which tells of a certain rabbi's son who spends all his time studying. A key Hasidic tenet is that knowledge without passion and inspiration is meaningless, and that is the case with this young man, who 'carried with him a sense of emptiness whose cause he did not know. Learning and praying held no appeal for him.' The remedy, his friends suggest, is to visit a tzaddik, a Hasidic holy man, who could supply the fervour he lacks. But his father, typically of the rabbinic establishment at the time, looks down on the Hasidim as low-born and ignorant: 'Why would you ever want to go to such riffraff when you are more learned than he is and come from a far better family?'

There is no question where the reader's sympathy is supposed to lie in this contest of wills: we are rooting for the son to defy his father and visit the tzaddik. The story consists of a series of attempts by the son to do just that, each of which is thwarted by what appears to be a sign from God. First, the father and son set out to visit the tzaddik and their wagon overturns, which the father takes as a warning that 'this journey is not meant to be'. When the son 'again felt something lacking' and insists they try again, the wagon's axles break. On the third attempt, the father and son stop at an inn and get into conversation with a merchant. When they reveal that they are on the way to the tzaddik, the merchant declares that he personally witnessed the holy man commit a sin: 'this was no respectable saint but rather an impious rogue.' This is surely another clear sign, and the father and son break off their journey.

Before he can visit the tzaddik, the son dies. Soon after, he appears to his father the rabbi in a dream, full of reproaches, and says that the tzaddik can explain why he is so angry. The father brushes it off, but when he has the same dream three times in a row, he finally decides to do as he was told and visit the tzaddik. On the way, he runs into the merchant who had dissuaded him. Only now the merchant reveals himself as a demon, saying that he was responsible for all their mishaps. He explains that the son 'had attained the brilliance of the lesser luminary', the moon, and the tzaddik was as brilliant as the sun, so 'if the two of them were to have joined together, the Messiah would have come'. By playing on the rabbi's resistance and arrogance, the demon prevented the meeting from taking place and ensured that the world would remain in its fallen state.

The pro-Hasidic message of this story is easy to understand: One must trust in the tzaddik and not the rabbi. No matter how respectable a rabbi may be, no matter how many good reasons he can give for not enlisting in the Hasidic ranks, he is still working against God's will. A Hasid's relationship with his spiritual leader is more important even than a son's with his father.

Yet Nachman's story also has a more troubling implication. After all, the rabbi continually asks God for signs about whether his son should visit the tzaddik, and he receives them. His only failure lies in not realizing that those signs actually come from Satan, not God. But in a world where Satan can counterfeit God so effectively, how can anyone tell a true prophet from a false one? This problem is as old as the Bible, and still just as subversive. If the supernatural is not the province of God alone, if there are evil powers in the universe who can shape our lives, then it becomes impossible to read the universe's language. The believer is adrift in a world of contradictory messages, with nothing but faith to guide him—in this case, the total faith in the tzaddik that Nachman demands.

It is when Nachman turns from this world to the next, from human beings to God, that the tales' uncanniness blossoms. That is what happens in 'Of a Humble King's Portrait', one of Nachman's most enigmatic and Kafka-like stories. Like many of them, it begins with a king; but this king is himself in search of another, greater king, who is known as both a mighty warrior and a 'man of truth and humility'. This humble king has never been seen, because his island kingdom is cut off from the world. The first king longs to get a portrait of the humble king, 'but no king possessed the portrait of the island king, because that king kept himself hidden from people, seated behind a curtain, and distant from his subjects'. So he sends a wise man as an emissary, charged with obtaining the humble king's likeness.

Now the story takes an unlikely turn, as Nachman focuses on a new subject—the nature of jokes. The wise man, arriving in the land of the humble king, decides that the best way to find out about the character of that land is to learn its jokes: 'if one needs to understand a thing's essence, one has to get a feel for the jokes about it.' All the jokes in the country, he discovers, are made up by one man, and when the wise man goes to see him, he realizes that the jokes are actually keys to the country's vices and sins: 'He saw all the kinds of derision and joking that went on, and he understood from them that the country was full of deception.'

This discovery presents a serious problem for the wise man. If the humble king is 'a man of truth', how is it that the country he rules is so corrupt? Determined to find an answer, the wise man makes it to the humble king's palace and lays out his indictment: 'Over whom are you king? Your country is overrun with lies, from start to finish. There is no truth in it whatsoever.' During all of this, he still can't see the king, who is hidden behind a curtain. But then the wise man changes tactics. It must be, he decides, that the humble king does know about the evil of his country, and that is why he hides—because he 'cannot bear to see [his] country's deceitfulness'. His seeming absence is actually what proves that he is a good ruler.

At this point, the wise man begins to praise the king in hyperbolic terms. But the king's humility is so great that the more praise he hears, the more he shrinks in size, until finally 'he had become nothing'. At this point, the nothing-sized king pulls back the curtain, eager to see the wise man who understands him so well. In doing so, he finally reveals his face, and 'the sage gazed upon it and went on to paint the king's portrait, which he brought to his own king'. And so the story ends.

In the original edition of the *Tales*, 'Of a Humble King's Portrait' is followed by a note from the editor, Rabbi Nathan, who explains that when Nachman first told it, he 'expressly said that he was revealing some hints and verses alluding to the mysteries in the stories… However, the mysteries of these stories extend far beyond the grasp of our knowledge.' The sense of Nachman's hidden depths is nowhere stronger than in this tale, which is so replete with paradoxes. A good king rules an evil kingdom; a great king is so humble that he can't abide praise. The sage makes a portrait of the king only once he has disappeared, so presumably the painting he brings home is blank, yet this blankness is somehow a true likeness.

It is these contradictions that make 'Of a Humble King's Portrait' so evocative. For it is clear that the humble king—the one whose reputation fills the world, but whom no one has ever seen—is Nachman's way of talking about God. God is constantly referred to as a king in the Bible and Jewish liturgy, and whenever a king appears in Nachman's tales there is a good chance that he is a stand-in for God. But if the humble king is God, then he is a God who rules over a world in disarray. Instead of making everything fair and orderly, he has withdrawn from the scene, leaving people so hardened and cynical that they joke about their own crimes.

God's absence from our world is one of the major themes of Kabbalah, and 'Of a Humble King's Portrait', like most of Nachman's stories, deals in Kabbalistic symbolism. In Kabbalistic terms, the ultimate reality of God is the *Eyn Sof*, the limitless, which cannot be grasped in human language or concepts. It is only once God ceases to take any form we can imagine or perceive that we encounter His essence, and so only a portrait of nothing can capture His likeness.

Lurianic Kabbalah offers an intricate cosmology explaining the stages of the universe's fall from wholeness, and many of its terms of art can be detected in Nachman's stories. But the emotional truth that this myth encodes is similar to the one expressed in the story of the fall of Adam, in Genesis. Our world was once perfect and now it is imperfect. Something has gone wrong in the very fabric of creation, which it is our duty to put right.

It is no coincidence that themes of falling and scattering should have become so central to Jewish thought. After all, Jewish history presents itself as a series of losses, descents, and catastrophes. As early as Deuteronomy, Moses envisioned the Jewish people losing their homeland and being sent into exile. This duly came to pass in the sixth century BCE, under the Babylonians, and again in the first century CE, under the Romans. Most of Jewish history has taken place in a condition of exile from the homeland. And within this exile the Jews experienced perpetual flights and exoduses, massacres and genocides. To live as a Jew is to live in a broken world. Nachman's mystical Hasidism offered the assurance that this world could be healed—that the power of the tzaddik could repair the universe, end the exile, bring the Messiah.

Nachman considered 'Of Seven Beggars', the last story he told before his death, to be his masterpiece. 'If I only told the world this one story, I would still be truly great,' he commented immodestly. It is certainly the most elaborate of the *Tales*, consisting of a series of nested stories. It begins by describing a king who transferred his kingdom to his only son, celebrating with a great feast. Yet this happiness is shadowed by the king's warning to his son that 'one day you will descend from the throne'.

This downfall comes about because the new king becomes obsessed with secular learning. Nachman lived at a time when the Haskalah, the Jewish Enlightenment, had only barely begun to penetrate Eastern Europe, yet he already foresaw a day when secularism would become the greatest challenge to traditional Jewish faith. The king's son, who grows so interested in worldly 'wisdom' that he becomes a heretic, represents the intellectuals whom Nachman feared would go astray. Still, the tale assures us that 'the general public was not influenced by this and did not, likewise, slip into heresy'.

Possibly as a result of the king's freethinking—though this is not made totally explicit—a disaster is visited on his land, and the entire population has to 'evacuate'. Nachman does not say exactly what the disaster is, which only heightens its power as a symbol: it can be taken as an allegory of Adam's fall, or of the exile of the Jewish people, or of the dispersal of the divine sparks. However we read it, this exodus sets the stage for the next part of the tale, which concerns two young children, a boy and a girl, who get lost in the chaos and end up alone in the forest. On the brink of starvation, they survive thanks to a series of seven beggars who pass by and give them bread. Each of these beggars is afflicted in a different way: the first is blind, the second is deaf, the third stammers, and so on. It is therefore an ambiguous blessing when each leaves the children with the words, 'May you be as I am.'

The two children survive, and when they grow up they decide to get married. The only thing missing to complete the happiness of the wedding feast, they say, is the presence of the seven beggars who long ago saved their lives. No sooner have they said so than the beggars appear, one by one, and reveal that what the children initially took to be a handicap was, in fact, the disguise of a great virtue. The blind beggar explains that he is not really blind; he sees nothing because worldly things have no value to him: 'The whole world rushes before me in the blink of an eye, a flash.' The deaf beggar is able to hear, but chooses not to because the world is full of complaint and misery: 'Everyone bemoans what he lacks.'

And so on for the next four beggars—the one with a speech defect, the one with a crooked neck, the hunchback, and the one with no hands. Allegorically, each of the seven beggars can be identified with one of the Biblical leaders of Israel, from Abraham down to King David. Kabbalistically, they can be identified with the parts of Adam Kadmon, the cosmic man. But these additional levels of interpretation don't obscure the story's plain meaning, which is moral and spiritual: in a fallen world, what looks like weakness is often really strength, and vice versa.

When each of the beggars arrives at the wedding to bestow a blessing, he also tells a story; and these stories-within-the-story form the heart of 'Of Seven Beggars'. Each is a poetic fable that illuminates a spiritual truth, but the most moving may be the one told by the third beggar. In his story, 'the heart of the world' stands at one end of the earth and yearns for a spring atop a mountain at the opposite end. The heart 'cries out constantly in its desire to come to the spring', yet it doesn't dare set out on the journey, because at the first step it would lose sight of the mountain's peak; and the heart couldn't bear not seeing what it loves, even for a moment.

These poignant images of longing and separation can be parsed kabbalistically, with the lovers representing God's masculine and feminine principles, or Heaven and Earth, and the beggar who unites them representing the tzaddik. The story abounds in allusions to the Bible and the Zohar, as Nachman himself hinted: 'One who is versed in the sacred literature will be able to understand some of the allusions,' he said after telling it. But the power of 'Of Seven Beggars' can be felt even by a reader who misses these references, for Nachman is a master of the broken heart as much as of the broken world. For Judaism, the supremely religious emotion is longing, and Nachman's tales promise that this longing will be rewarded. But he does not actually give us that happy ending in 'Of Seven Beggars', since the story of the seventh beggar goes untold; Rabbi Nathan explains that we will not be worthy of hearing it 'until the Messiah comes'.

ADAM KIRSCH

THE
PODOLIAN
NIGHTS

FIRST TALE

Of the Loss of a Princess

*On the road I told a tale that
all those who heard it had
thoughts of turning
themselves
around.*

Here is the story:

ONCE THERE WAS a king. The king had six sons and one daughter. And this daughter was his pride and joy. He loved and cherished her very much and took great delight in her. One day he was with her someplace and he grew vexed with her. He let slip the words, To the Wicked One with you!

That night she went into her chamber and in the morning she was nowhere to be found.

So her father, the king, was distraught and began to search for her.

Seeing how greatly aggrieved the king was, the royal steward then rose and bade the king give him a servant and a horse and some money for expenses—and out he went to look high and low for her.

3

And he searched for her everywhere, for a very long time, until he found her.

Now he tells how the royal steward sought her until he found her.

The royal steward went searching for a very long while. Across wastelands and over fields and through forests, he looked and looked. Once, as he was crossing a barren wasteland, he saw a path that branched off to the side. He thought, Since I have been travelling so long in the wastelands and still have not found her, I shall go this way. Perhaps it will lead to some settlement.

He walked for some time until he saw a castle with many guards stationed in front. The castle was lovely to behold, and the guards stood arrayed in very fine rows. He was afraid the guards would not allow him to enter. But, he decided, I shall try.

He dismounted his horse and went to the castle, and he was let in. No one even stood in his way. He went from one chamber to the next, unimpeded by anyone. As he approached the keep, he saw a king wearing a crown sitting with many guards encircling him. Numerous musicians were playing instruments before him, and it was all very splendid and lovely. Neither the king nor anyone there even so much as asked him a question.

He saw an array of fine delicacies. He walked over and helped himself to them. Then he went and rested in a nook, waiting to see what would happen next. He watched as the king called

4

for his queen to be brought to him and they went to fetch her. There was a mighty din and a great fanfare as the musicians piped up, playing and singing as the queen was escorted in. A throne was carried in and she was seated next to him. It was the princess!

When the queen looked about, she spied someone resting in a nook and, recognizing him, rose from the throne and approached. Laying her hand upon him, she asked, Do you know me?

He answered: Yes, I know you. You are the princess who has gone missing.

He asked her how she came to be here and she replied, Because my papa blurted out those words—To the Wicked One with you—and this place is a wicked one indeed.

He told her that her father was distraught and that he had searched all these many years for her. He asked, But how can I take you out of here?

She answered, You cannot get me out without first finding a place for yourself to settle for one year. And for the entirety of that year, you must steadfastly long for my deliverance. Whenever you have a moment to spare, you must do nothing but yearn and hope for my release. Then, on the very last day of the year, you must fast. You must fast and also refrain from sleeping from that dawn until the next.

And he went and did just that. When the end of the year came, on the very last day, he fasted and did not sleep. He got up and headed off to see the princess in order to take her out of there at last, when he caught sight of a tree upon which grew very lovely apples. He was overcome with craving and went and ate of them. As soon as he tasted the apple, he dropped to the ground and fell into a deep slumber. And he slept an exceedingly long time. His servant went to wake him but found that he could not.

Later, when he woke from his sleep, he asked his servant, Where in the world am I?

So his servant told him the whole tale: You have been asleep for a very long time; it has been years already since you fell asleep. And I have had to support myself selling these fruits.

He was filled with sorrow and headed straight off to find the princess.

She, too, was filled with sorrow and lamented to him, On account of one day, you have lost. Since you were unable to restrain yourself for one single day and ate the apple, you failed. For had you come that day, you could have gotten me out of here. Not eating is, indeed, a difficult thing, especially on the very last day, when temptation is most powerful. So now, once more, you must find yourself a place and settle there for yet another year. And, this time, on the very last day, you will be permitted to eat, but you must not sleep. For surely sleep is the key.

So he went and did just that. On the last day he headed out and, as he was walking, he saw a spring. This spring appeared to be flowing red and had the fragrance of wine. So he asked his servant: Have you ever seen such a thing? Here is a spring that should run with water but it looks red and is redolent of wine. He went and tasted of the spring and thereupon fell into a deep slumber. And he slept for many years, a good seventy of them.

After he dropped into sleep, a large number of guards passed by, with heavy cloaks trailing behind them as they went. The servant hid himself out of the guards' sight. Following behind them went a carriage, in which the princess was seated. She came to a halt beside him and, recognizing him, alighted and tried hard to rouse him. But she could not awaken him and began to lament, Oh, all the many trials and tribulations and so much trouble and travail, so many years of exhausting struggle, toiling to get me out of here, and at last when the day arrives on which you were to take me away, you forfeited everything. She wept bitterly then said, Such a great pity for you and for me. I have been here for such a long time… And on she went in this manner. Then she unwrapped the shawl from around her head and with her own tears she wrote upon it. When she finished, she laid it down beside him, rose, and, returning to her carriage, rode off.

When he eventually awoke, he asked his servant, Where in the world am I? And he told him the whole tale: how the guards had marched by and about the arrival of the carriage and how she had wept over him and bawled about what a terrible pity it was for the two of them. Then he caught sight of the shawl lying next to him and he asked where it came from. His servant told him that she had left it there and had written upon it with her tears. He took the shawl from him and, holding it to the sun, he began to make out the letters. He read the grief and sorrow that she had set down upon it. There it was written that now she would no longer be found in the same palace as before. He would have to search for a golden mountain with a pearl palace—There, she wrote, you will find me.

He took leave of his servant and headed off to search for her alone. He went searching for many years. He reckoned that it would be highly unlikely to find such a golden mountain with a pearl palace near a town, as he was well versed in geography and cartography. Therefore, he said, I shall go into the wastelands to search.

So he went searching in the wastelands for many, many years. One day, he observed an enormous man, whose size was simply not human, carrying an enormous tree larger than any tree to be found in a town. And this man asked him, Who are you?

He answered, I am a man.

Astonished, the enormous man said, I have been in the wasteland for a long, long time and I have never seen a man.

So he told him his entire tale and of how he was now searching for a golden mountain with a pearl palace.

Certainly there is no such thing, he answered him, rejecting what he had said, and maintained that he had been misled by nonsense, for surely there was no such place.

At that, the royal steward began to cry in earnest, as he countered that such a place most certainly did exist. Indeed, it must be somewhere.

But the extraordinary man reproved him, saying, You have been misled by nonsense, but since you insist, as I am the warden of all animals, I shall assemble all of the animals for you; they roam over the entire world so perhaps one of them might know of such a mountain with such a palace.

So he gathered all the animals, from the smallest to the greatest, and asked them. All of them responded that they had not. And he said, Can you not see? You have been misled by nonsense and you should heed me and turn around since you will surely never find such a place because it does not exist in this world.

But the royal steward continued to insist that such a place must certainly exist.

The extraordinary man then told the royal steward, I have a brother in the wasteland who is the warden of all the birds; perhaps they might know since they fly high in the air. Maybe they have seen this mountain with this palace. Go to him and say that I have sent you.

He continued walking for many, many years, looking for him, when at last he encountered an enormous man as before. This man also carried an enormous tree and also inquired who he was, just as the first had. So he responded by telling him the whole tale and how his brother had sent him to him.

He, too, countered that certainly there was no such place, but the royal steward maintained that there certainly was. He told him, As I am the warden of all the birds, I shall call them all to find out if they know.

So he assembled all of the birds and asked each of them, from the smallest to the greatest. They responded that they did not know of any such mountain or palace.

You see, he told him, there is certainly no such place in the world and you should heed me and turn around, for it surely does not exist.

But the royal steward held firm and said, Such a place does indeed exist in this world.

9

He responded, Further on in the wasteland lives my brother who is the warden of all the winds. Since the winds run their course over the whole world, perhaps they know.

So he went off searching for many, many years until, again, he encountered an enormous man. This man also carried an enormous tree and he approached and enquired. He responded with the whole story, just as before. And the man also tried to disabuse him. The royal steward again besought him. So he told him he would call together all the winds for him to ask. Thereupon he summoned them, and all of the winds came and he asked each of them. But nary a one knew of the mountain with the palace. The man said to the royal steward, Do you see how you have been told nonsense?

At that the royal steward began to weep, saying, But I know with certainty that it does exist.

Then he saw another wind arrive and the warden scolded it, Why have you come so late? When I give an order, all the winds should obey. Why did you not come with the others?

It replied, I was delayed because I had to deliver a princess to a golden mountain with a pearl palace. And upon hearing this the royal steward rejoiced.

The warden of the winds asked the wind, How precious are things there?

It responded, There, everything is most precious.

The warden of the winds turned then to the royal steward and said, Since you have searched for so long and gone through so many trials and tribulations, you might now be hindered due to a lack of money. Therefore, I will give you a vessel that, whenever you reach your hand into it, you may draw out money.

Then he ordered the wind to take him. And it brought him to the gate, where guards stood and refused to let him into the town. So he reached his hand into the vessel and extracted money to bribe them. Then he entered the town and it was a lovely town.

He found his way to a landlord and arranged for his room and board, for he might need to linger there for some time to assess, with wisdom and reason, how to extricate her.

How he managed to get
her out, he did not tell.

And at long last, he brought her out.
Amen Selah

SECOND TALE

Of a King and an Emperor

A story:

O NCE THERE WAS an emperor. This emperor had no
children. There was, at the same time, a king who also
had no children.

The emperor set off into the world to see whether he could find
some care or cure for his childlessness. The king likewise set off.

The two of them arrived at an inn and neither knew the other.
The emperor did, however, recognize the king's regal bearing
and asked him about it. The king averred that he was, indeed,
a king. The king had similarly discerned a noble comportment
in the emperor, who acknowledged it. They each told the other
they were travelling to find a way to end their childless state. They
came to an agreement that if, upon their return home, one of
their wives should bear a son and the other a daughter the two
would be betrothed.

The emperor travelled home and had a daughter, and the
king travelled home and had a son. Yet the betrothal was forgotten by all. The emperor sent his daughter off to study. The king,
too, sent his son off to study. The two children had been sent to
the very same tutor. They fell deeply in love and resolved to be

married. The king's son took a ring, placed it on her finger, and the two were betrothed.

Soon thereafter, the emperor sent for his daughter and brought her home, and the king sent for his son and brought him home. Offers of marriage were made to the emperor's daughter, but she did not want to entertain them because of her pledge to the prince. The king's son longed for her, and the emperor's daughter was in constant sorrow. The emperor would take his daughter for walks through his courtyards and palaces, showing her all of their splendour, but she remained forlorn. For his part, the king's son longed for her with such intensity that he became ill. When people asked, What has made you ill?, he did not wish to reply. So they turned to his attendant, who had been serving the prince when he was studying with his tutor: Perhaps you might explain it?

He answered, Indeed, I know. And he told them why the prince was sick.

It suddenly occurred to the king that he had long ago made a marriage arrangement with the emperor. So he wrote to the emperor that he should expect a wedding because their fore-going agreement was still in effect. The emperor, however, did not want this match, but he could not refuse, so he wrote back that the king should send his son to determine whether he was capable of becoming the ruler of a country, and, if so, he would give him his daughter in marriage. The king sent him his son. The emperor then seated him in a chamber and entrusted him with papers of state in order to see whether he would be able to govern.

The prince longed desperately to see the emperor's daughter but could not do so. One time, as he was walking by a wall of mirrored glass, he caught a glimpse of her and swooned. She came to him and cheered him, telling him she wanted nothing to do with any marriage offers because of her pledge to him.

He said to her, What can we do? Your father does not want me for you.

She replied, Even so!

In spite of it all, she clung to him.

The two decided to sail away. They hired a boat and set out to sea. Thus they sailed and made their way to a wooded shore. They entered the forest. The emperor's daughter took off her ring and gave it to the prince for safekeeping. She then lay down to sleep. After some time, when the prince saw she was stirring, he put the ring down next to her.

Once they had returned to the ship, she realized they had forgotten the ring, so she sent him back for it. He entered the forest but could not find the place they had been, so he went deeper into the woods. He still could not find the ring, so he searched high and low until he got lost and was unable to find his way back. She went out in search of him and also lost her way. He wandered and wandered, and then suddenly spied a path, which took him to a settlement. There was nothing he could do so he stayed and became a servant.

She, too, wandered lost and decided she would come to rest by the sea. She went to the seashore where there were fruit trees, and there she stayed, living off the fruit. By day she wandered the coast in case she might encounter someone, and by night she climbed into the treetops to shelter from wild beasts.

And it came to pass...

Once there was a very wealthy merchant who had business interests around the world. He had an only son. And the merchant was already old.

One time the son said to his father, As you are old and I am still young, yet your factotums pay me no heed, what will happen when you die and I am left on my own? I will not know what to do. Give me a ship loaded with goods so I can set out to sea and gain experience in trade.

So his father gave him a ship freighted with goods and he set off and travelled abroad, selling his goods and buying others, and becoming very successful.

While he was at sea, he descried the woods where the emperor's daughter dwelt. The sailors thought it was a settlement and headed for it. When they drew nearer and saw it was only trees, they wanted to turn around. In the meantime, the merchant's son looked into the sea and saw a tree, and sitting up in the tree was something very like a person. He thought perhaps he was mistaken, so he told the rest of his crew. They looked and they, too, saw something like a person up in the tree. So they decided they would investigate and sent one of them ashore in a little boat. The crew kept lookout on the sea to guide their envoy to the tree. The envoy set off and saw that there was indeed a person in the tree, which he signalled back to them. Then the merchant's son went and saw the emperor's daughter sitting in the tree. He told her to come down, but she told him she would not board the ship unless he promised he would not lay a hand on her until they returned home and were lawfully wed. He promised, and she boarded his ship.

He discerned that she was a gifted musician and could speak several languages, so he was pleased they had chanced to meet.

As they neared his home, she told him that the proper thing to do would be for him to go home and inform his father and relatives and close friends that since he was escorting a noblewoman, they should all come out to welcome her. And as she had earlier insisted that he not ask who she was until their wedding, only then would he discover her identity. He acceded to her request.

She went on to tell him, The proper thing to do would be for you to let all your ship's crew carouse so they might become better acquainted with the kind of woman their merchant was to marry.

He obeyed and took the fine wine he had aboard ship and gave it to them, and they became very drunk. He then went home to inform his father and friends. The sailors, meanwhile, grew increasingly inebriated and left the ship and fell down drunk.

While he and his entire family were preparing to go out to welcome her, she had in the meantime returned to the ship, unmoored it, unfurled its sails and sailed away. When the whole family arrived where the ship had been and found no one there, the merchant grew very angry at his son. His son exclaimed, Believe me! I did bring a ship full of goods!

But they did not see one. So he told them, Go ask the sailors. He went to ask them but they lay around drunk.

Later, once they were up and about again, they were questioned and had no idea what had happened to them. They knew they had brought in a ship loaded with goods but were unaware of where it was now. The merchant once more grew furious with his son and drove him out of his house, not wishing to set eyes on him again.

His son became a fugitive and a vagabond, and the emperor's daughter sailed upon the sea.

And it came to pass...

Once there was a king. This king built palaces by the sea because the sea air pleased him, as did the ships that passed. The emperor's daughter was sailing by and neared the king's palace. The king glanced at the ship and noticed that it was moving without oars and that there was no crew aboard. He thought he was mistaken, so he ordered his retinue to look. They looked and saw the same thing.

As she approached the palace she thought, Such a palace matters nothing to me, and started to turn around to leave. The king, however, sent word to her and had her turn back around. He brought her into his home. The king had no wife because he found himself in an impossible bind: whomever he wanted did not want him, and vice versa. When the emperor's daughter came to him she told him to swear that he would not lay a hand on her until they were lawfully wed. He swore. Then she told him that the proper thing to do would be neither to open her ship nor even to touch it but to leave it anchored at sea until the wedding for all to see the extent of the goods she had brought.

18

Then no one could say he had married some commoner. This he also promised.

The king wrote to the rulers of every country, inviting them to the wedding. He built a suite of chambers for her. She demanded that eleven noblewomen be brought to attend her. The king so ordered, and eleven ladies, the daughters of great lords, were sent to her. A chamber was supplied to each of them, and they would come to her at court and play music and games with her.

Once she told them she wanted to go to sea with them, and so they went and there they played. She told them she wanted to treat them to the fine wine she had on board her ship, so she gave them some of the wine she had in the hold. They became drunk and fell down, and there they lay all around. She then went and unmoored the ship, unfurled its sails and fled.

The king and his retinue looked and saw that the ship was no longer there, and they became terribly frightened. The king told them, See to it that you do not let her know straight away that her ship is gone because she will be greatly distressed.

The king did not know that it was she who had fled, for he thought she was still in her chamber, and she might think the king had gifted her ship away. Instead, one of the ladies should be sent to inform her judiciously. Pages were sent to one of the ladies' chambers, but no one was there. So they went to another chamber, and likewise, no one was there either. And so it was that in all eleven chambers there was no lady to be found. The king and his retinue deliberated, deciding that an old dowager should be sent to her that night to inform her. The dowager went to her chamber, but again no one was there. They all grew alarmed.

19

Meanwhile, the ladies' fathers realized they had received no word from their daughters. They sent word but received no replies. So they set off and travelled themselves to see them but found none of their daughters. They grew very angry and wanted to banish the king, because they were royal ministers. They considered: Is the king so guilty that he merits banishment? After all, this was not his fault. But, it was determined that they would indeed spurn his kingship and exile him. They deposed him and cast him out. And he went away.

The emperor's daughter who had fled was travelling in the ship. Then the ladies awoke and started playing with her as they had before because they did not realize the ship had already departed the coast. Later, however, they said to her, Let us return home.

She asked them, May we just linger here awhile?

A squall overtook them. They said, Let us turn back.

She revealed to them that they had long left the coast behind.

They asked her, Why have you done this?

She said she had been afraid lest the ship be smashed to pieces because of the squall. That was why she had to do so.

They continued upon the sea, the emperor's daughter and the eleven ladies, often playing music on their instruments, when they chanced upon a palace.

The ladies said to her, Let us go to that palace.

She did not want to do so and said she regretted having come near the palace at all.

Some time thereafter they spied something like an isle in the sea and they approached it. There were twelve bandits on the isle and these bandits wanted to kill them.

She asked, Who is the greatest among you?, and they pointed him out.

So she asked him, What is it you do?

He told her they were bandits, and she said to him, We, too, are bandits. But you are bandits by might, while we are bandits by wisdom, for we have studied many languages and play musical instruments. What do you gain by killing us? It would be better to take us as your wives, and you will also be acquiring a great fortune.

She then showed them what was in the ship, for the ship was well laden with the merchant's son's fortune. The bandits were placated by her words and showed the women their own riches, leading them to all of their hidden lairs. They decided not to marry them all at once but rather one after the other, and, furthermore, each of them was to choose the lady best suited to him and his own character.

After that, she told them she would treat them to the finest wine she had in the ship, wine which she never touched and which she kept hidden until God revealed her intended. She served them the wine in twelve goblets and asked each one to drink to the health of all twelve. They drank and became drunk and fell down.

She then called out to the rest of the ladies, Go now each of you and slaughter your husband.

They went and killed them all. Then they found their great riches, far surpassing those of a king, and decided to take neither copper nor silver but only gold and jewels. They cast everything that was not valuable overboard and loaded the ship with the precious goods, all the gold and jewels they had found there on the isle. They also decided not to dress like women and tailored men's clothes for themselves in a fashionable European style and sailed away.

And it came to pass...

Once there was a king. This king had an only son whom he had married off and to whom he entrusted his kingdom.

One time he said to his father he wanted to go for a cruise with his wife so she could get accustomed to the sea air. They might have to escape to sea at some point so he wanted her to get used to the sea's climes.

The prince, his wife and his royal ministers set off upon a ship and were very merry and frolicsome there. It was then suggested they should all take off their clothes and so they did, leaving on nothing but their undergarments. Then each one tried to see who could climb the mast. The prince scaled the mast.

Meantime, the emperor's daughter had arrived in her ship and spied the ship of the prince and his ministers. At first she was afraid to approach, so she drew nearer little by little. She saw them disporting themselves and realized these were no pirates, so she sailed closer. The emperor's daughter said to her entourage, I can knock that pate down into the sea. (For the prince who had scaled the mast had a bald spot on his head.)

They said to her, How is that possible? We are so far away.

She told them she had a burning glass and with it she could take him down. She bided her time until he had reached the very top of the mast, because as long as he was in the middle of the

22

mast when he fell he would fall into the ship, but if he were at the very top when he fell he would plummet into the water. So she waited for him to reach the tip of the mast. Then she took the burning glass and directed it towards his skull until his brain was scorched and he fell into the sea.

His fall caused a great commotion on his ship, and they did not know what to do. How could they return home? The king would die of grief. So they decided to make for the ship they had seen in the distance that belonged to the emperor's daughter, as it might have a doctor on board who could treat him. They approached and told the people aboard the emperor's daughter's ship not to fear because they meant them no harm. They asked if there were a doctor among them with whom they might consult. They told them the whole story of how the prince had fallen into the sea.

The emperor's daughter told them to pull him out of the sea. So they went and found him and hauled him out. The emperor's daughter then took his pulse and said, His brain has been scorched.

They went and opened his skull and saw that it was indeed as she had said. They were astounded, for it was such a wonder that the doctor, that is, the emperor's daughter, could have hit on exactly the right cause and they asked whether she would accompany them back to their home and become the king's physician and a very eminent person. She did not wish to do so and told them she was no doctor but she simply understood such matters well.

The people on the prince's ship were reluctant to return home so the two ships sailed on together. The royal ministers aboard were much taken with the idea that the late prince's wife should marry the doctor—the emperor's daughter, who was dressed as a man and whom they thought a doctor—because they understood him to be a very wise man. Now they wished their royal consort to marry the doctor and for him to become their king. As for their old king, the late prince's father, they would kill him. They were reluctant at first to tell the royal consort to marry a doctor, but she was well pleased at the idea. She was afraid, however, of her countrymen lest they not want him to be king. They decided to hold a feast aboard the ship so that amidst the drinking, surrounded by merrymaking, they would be able to discuss it. So they planned a feast for all on a particular date. When the day came, the doctor—that is, the emperor's daughter—joined the revelry. He gave them the fine wine he had and they became drunk.

Amidst the merrymaking, the royal ministers said, How lovely it would be if the queen married the doctor.

The doctor replied, It would certainly be very lovely indeed, but one should not speak with a drunken tongue.

The royal consort added, It would be very lovely to marry the doctor, but the country would have to agree.

The doctor repeated, It would certainly be very lovely, but one should not speak with a drunken tongue.

Later, once they had sobered up, the ministers remembered what had been said and were ashamed of having spoken in such a way to a royal consort. But they reflected, She herself said this to you. And the queen was equally ashamed before them. But, she reconsidered, they themselves have said this to you as well. In the meantime, they began discussing the situation. It was decided

24

that the royal consort should marry the doctor, and they went home to their country.

When their countrymen beheld them returning they were overjoyed, as it had been so long since the prince had left on his cruise. They had not known where he was and the old king had passed away before their return. When their countrymen saw, however, that the prince who was now their presumptive king was not there, they asked, Where is our king?

Thereupon they told them the whole tale, how the prince had been long dead and how they had already appointed a new king who was with them—namely, the doctor, who was the emperor's daughter. Their countrymen rejoiced at having a new king.

The king ordered it be proclaimed in all the lands that whosoever one may be, whether foreigner or fugitive, exile or outcast, let them be invited to the wedding, let none be lacking, and they would be given great gifts. And the king went on to order that fountains be built everywhere around the whole city so that everyone would be able to have a drink. One should not have to go too far in order to have a drink, but rather one should be able to find a fountain nearby. The king also ordered his likeness to be painted on each of the fountains. Guards were to be stationed at each of the fountains, and if anyone were to stare too intensely at the likeness or grimace, he should be seized and thrown in prison. Everything was done as commanded.

Among those that came to the wedding, these three arrived: the first prince, who was the proper bridegroom of the emperor's daughter who was now the king; the merchant's son, whose father had cast him out when the emperor's daughter had sailed away;

and the king who had been deposed and exiled, similarly on account of the emperor's daughter, who had absconded with the eleven ladies. Each one of the three recognized her likeness on the fountains. As they stared at it and remembered, their faces showed their distress. They were seized and thrown into prison.

At the wedding celebration, the new king ordered the prisoners brought before him. All three were hauled in. She recognized them, but they did not recognize her because she was dressed as a man.

The emperor's daughter spoke, saying, You, King, were exiled on account of the eleven ladies who were lost. Here now, take your ladies and return to your country and your kingship.

You, Merchant, were cast out by your father on account of the ship and the goods that were lost. Here now, take your ship and all your goods; and since your fortune has been unattainable for so long, you now have many times more riches in your ship than you had before.

And you, Prince, she said to the first prince, who was truly her bridegroom, Come hither. Let us go home.

And they returned home.

Amen and Amen

THIRD TALE

Of a Lame Man

A story:

O NCE THERE WAS a wise man who, before he died, called
for his children and family and left them his will wherein
they were admonished to keep the trees watered. You may
busy yourselves with other vocations, he cautioned them, but
always be heedful of keeping the trees watered. Then the wise
man died.

Among the children he left behind was a lame son who was
unable to walk. He could stand, but could not walk. His brothers provided for his support. They provided so much, in fact,
that he had more than enough. So, little by little, he had saved
everything that was left over after his needs were met until he
had amassed quite a lot of money. He reflected, Why should I
keep living off their charity? It would be better for me to start
up in business even if I cannot walk.

So he decided to hire a wagon, a faithful servant and a driver
and to ride with them to the great fair in Leipzig. That way he
could conduct business despite his lameness.

When his family heard this they were very pleased, and
they said to one another, Why should we keep providing for his

support? It would be better to let him make a living for himself. They contributed some more money so he could go into business on his own. Which he did, hiring a wagon, a faithful servant and a driver. They set off and passed by an inn, where the servant suggested they spend the night. The lame man, however, did not want to follow this suggestion and prevailed on them to keep going. They travelled on and got lost in a forest, where they were set upon by bandits.

Some time earlier, there had been a famine. A man came to a city and announced that whoever wanted to eat should come to see him. Many people went to see him, so he was able to select which people would and would not be of use to him. Some of these he put off. To one he said, You should be a craftsman. To another he said, You should work in a mill. In this way he chose only the cleverest young men and these he led into the forest where he convinced them to become bandits. He cajoled, Since the roads lead from here to Leipzig and Breslau and other centres of commerce as well, merchants all travel this way. We will rob them and take their money. That was how these bandits came to set upon the lame man and his hirelings.

The servant and the driver were able to flee, so they did. But the lame man remained in the wagon. The bandits approached him and seized the chest with his money. They asked him, Why are you just sitting there? He answered that he was unable to walk. So they robbed him of his money chest and his horses, leaving him in the wagon. The servant and the driver who had fled reckoned that since the lame man's family had advanced them their pay, how could they show their faces at home again?

They might be put in chains. It would be better to stay where they were and remain a servant and a driver.

As for the man who was unable to walk and remained in the cart, as long as he had the biscuits he had brought from home he could eat. Later, once the biscuits had run out and he had nothing to eat, he considered what to do. He threw himself off the wagon so he could eat grass. He then spent the night alone in the field, and he was very frightened. His strength so flagged that he could not pull himself up and could only crawl along. As long as he could reach out for the grass around him and eat, he ate. When the grass around him ran out and he could not reach any more, he crawled further on and continued to graze. For some while he went on eating grass in this way.

One time he came upon a herb that he had never eaten before. This herb very much pleased him. He had spent a great deal of time eating herbs and could recognize them all, but this herb was unlike any he had seen before. So he decided to pull it out by the roots, and there beneath its roots was a jewel. This particular jewel had four sides, and each side bore a unique enchantment. On one side it was written that whosoever held it by that particular side would be transported whither day and night come together, that is, where the sun and the moon meet. When he pulled that herb out by the roots he happened to be holding the jewel by that very side and was whisked straight away to where day and night come together.

He looked around and saw he was at the meeting place of the sun and the moon. He heard the two talking, and the sun was fretting, There is a tree with a great many branches, fruit and leaves. Each branch and fruit and leaf has its own enchantment. One brings children, another brings livelihood; this one heals one illness, that one heals another. Each little piece of the tree is adept at one particular thing. If only this tree were watered, it would be a very effective tree. Yet not only am I not able to water it, but my rays shine down and dry it out.

The moon replied, Your worries are strange enough, but let me tell you about mine. I have a thousand mountains. And around those thousand mountains are yet another thousand mountains. This is the Lair of the Demons. The demons there have chickens' legs, which lack strength, so they sap strength from the legs of others, including mine. And now I have no strength left in my own legs. Once I had some dust, though, which is a cure for my legs, but along the wind came and blew it away.

So that is your problem? I know the cure for that. There is a path from which many smaller paths branch off. One is the path for tzaddikim. Whoever walks on this path, with every footfall on the dust strewn there, behold: he becomes a tzaddik. There is also a path for heretics. Whoever walks on that path, with every footfall on its dust he becomes a heretic. And similarly, there is a path for lunatics. There are, in this way, many such smaller paths. On another one, there are tzaddikim who walk their path of mortification led in chains and goaded on by overlords. These tzaddikim walk until they have no strength left in their legs. But when the dust of one of these paths is strewn beneath their steps, strength returns to their legs. Therefore you should go there where this dust abounds and you will find the cure for your legs.

The lame man overheard all of this.

Thereupon, he took a look at the other side of the jewel and saw written there that whosoever held it by that particular side would be transported to a path that branched into many smaller paths. So he held it by that side and was whisked away to that place. He placed his feet on the path whose dust was a cure for the legs and was instantly healed. So he went and collected dust from every path, placing each in its own particular pouch, and he took these pouches away with him.

After some deliberation, he decided to return to the forest where he had been robbed. When he arrived he selected a tall tree close to the road the bandits took. He mixed together the dust for the tzaddikim with the dust for the lunatics and spread it on the road. Then he climbed the tree and perched there to wait and see what would happen.

He spied the bandits heading on their way, having been dispatched to go robbing by their chief. When the bandits came to the road and set foot on the dust, they turned instantly into pious tzaddikim and wailed, ruing all their days of thievery and murder. Yet as the dust had also been mixed with the dust for the lunatics, they became deranged tzaddikim and started fighting with one another. One said, It is your fault that we murdered people. And another said, No, it is your fault.

They fought in this way until they had all killed each other. Then the bandits' chief sent out more bandits, and the same thing happened: they all killed one another. This happened several more times until the lot of them had been killed off and the formerly lame man in the tree reckoned there were no bandits left except their chief and one other. So he came down out of the tree and swept the dust from the road and spread only the dust for the tzaddikim instead. He went back up into the tree to perch.

The bandits' chief was nonplussed at the fact that he kept sending out bandits yet none of them returned. So he thought for a while before heading out himself with his sole remaining henchman. The moment his feet met the road he instantly turned into a tzaddik and started wailing at his companion, ruing all his murder and thievery. He was assiduous in his penitence and felt deep remorse.

When the formerly lame man saw the degree of the chief's remorse and the ardour of his atonement, he came down out of the tree. Spying a man, the chief began yelling, Alas for me! I have done so much. Help me! How can I ever make amends?

The formerly lame man replied, First, return the chest with my money that you stole.

The bandits had kept an inventory of each of their robberies, including when they had taken place and from whom they had stolen.

The chief said, I will return it to you immediately. I will even include all of my plundered treasures so long as you give me a penance to perform.

Your penance, he replied, is to go into the city and cry out your confession: I am the one who earlier announced for the hungry to come see me and from them I recruited bandits, who robbed and murdered many souls. That is your penance.

The bandits' chief handed over all his treasures to the once lame man. He accompanied him into the city, and there the chief did as he was bidden. It was adjudged that, since he had murdered so many souls, he was to be hanged to serve as a lesson for others.

Then the formerly lame man decided to go to the two thousand mountains the moon had spoken of to see what was happening there. When he was still at a distance from the mountains he could see there were myriads and multitudes of demon families, for they were fruitful and multiplied, having children just as people do. He saw their king seated upon a throne the likes of which no man born of woman had ever sat upon. He saw the demons capering and making jokes. One bantered about how he had maimed a baby; another quipped about how he had mangled someone's hand; and yet another wisecracked about how he had mutilated a human's foot. And there was other joking to boot.

Meantime, the formerly lame man spied a demon father and mother walking and crying. When another demon encountered them and asked, Why are you crying?, they replied that they had a son who had the habit of setting out and then returning at a particular time. Now, however, he had been gone for a long while and had not yet returned. So the parents were brought to the demon king who ordered messengers dispatched throughout the world to find him. When the father and mother returned from the king they came across a childhood friend of their son. He asked them, Why are you crying? So they told him, to which he replied, Let me tell you:

Your son and I had an islet in the sea, which was our own little playground. But the king who owned the islet came and wanted to build a palace there and went and laid a foundation for

33

it. So your son said to me, Let's teach him a lesson. So we went and sapped him of his strength. The king employed numerous physicians but none could help him, so he started consulting with sorcerers. There was one sorcerer who knew your lineage of demons but was unfamiliar with mine. Since a human's knowledge of a demon's lineage gives him power over that particular demon clan, he went and captured your son, and he tortured him harshly. But he could do nothing to me.

This young demon was brought to the demon king and he told the king the whole story. The demon king said, Let that king's strength be returned to him. The young demon replied, I do not have it. There was another demon among us who lacked strength, so we gave the king's strength to him.

The demon king answered, Then let that demon's strength be taken away again and returned to the king.

He replied, But that demon has since become a cloud.

The demon king then said, Let the cloud be summoned and brought here. So a messenger was sent for him.

The formerly lame man thought to himself, Let me go and find out how a cloud is made from a demon.

He followed the messenger and arrived at the city where the cloud was. He asked the city folk, Why is there a cloud looming over your city?

They replied, There was never a cloud here before, but not long ago a cloud came and covered the city.

Then the messenger came and summoned the cloud, and they headed back to the demon king together. The formerly lame man decided to follow them to listen in on what they were talking about. He heard the messenger ask the cloud, How is it that you became a cloud? The cloud replied, I will tell you the story.

Once there was a sage. The emperor of the sage's country was a formidable heretic and had made unbelievers of his entire country. So the sage gathered all his family together and said to them, Surely you see that the emperor is a formidable heretic and he has made all the people of this country unbelievers, even some members of our own family. Let us therefore decamp to the wastelands where we may keep our faith in Blessed God.

They agreed. So the sage uttered a spell, which whisked them all away to a wasteland. This wasteland was not to his liking so he again uttered a spell, and they were borne away to a different wasteland. This wasteland was not to his liking either, so once more he uttered a spell, and they were brought to yet another wasteland. This time the wasteland was to his liking. This wasteland was close to the two thousand mountains and our demon lair. So the sage went and traced a magic circle around their encampment so that the nearby demons would not be able to enter it.

There is a tree, the cloud continued, that were it to be watered all of us demons would be obliterated. So some of us keep eternal watch over it, and day and night other demons dig away at a trench around the tree to prevent any water from getting to it.

The messenger asked the cloud, Why do they need to keep digging away there day and night? Would it not be enough for them just to dig one deep trench so the water would never be able to reach the tree?

The cloud replied, Among us there are talebearers who foment conflict between one king and another, causing war. War produces earthquakes, which in turn repeatedly cause the earthworks of the trench to collapse, enabling water to reach the tree. That is why we must stand perpetual watch and keep digging.

Now, whenever a new demon king is named among us, we caper for him and make all kinds of jokes, and everyone is merry. This one jests about how he grievously maimed a baby and how the mother mourned it, and that one makes a different joke. It is the custom when our new king arrives at the festivities that he sallies forth with his royal ministers and attempts to uproot the tree, for it would be very good for all of us demons if there were no tree at all. The king steels himself to uproot the tree completely. As he rushes towards the tree, it shrieks at him at full volume. This frightens the king and he is forced to retreat.

Once, the cloud continued, there was a new demon king among us and there was the customary capering and joking for him. He arrived at the festivities and plucked up his courage, eager to uproot the tree utterly. He advanced with his ministers, steeled himself gravely, and sallied forth to uproot it. As he approached the tree, it shrieked loudly at him. He was stricken by fear and turned back. He grew exceedingly ill-tempered as he headed home.

Just then, he caught sight of the sage who had settled with his family close by. So he dispatched some of his men to do something about it and cause them harm. When the sage's family saw the demons coming, a terrible fear overtook them. The old sage said to them, Do not be afraid.

When the demons arrived they could not draw near because of the magic circle around the sage and his family. The king sent reinforcements, but they, too, were unable to come any closer. So the irascible king went himself, but he was similarly prevented from approaching them. So he asked the old sage to allow him inside. The old sage said, Because you have asked me I shall let you in. But it is not customary for a king to enter alone. Therefore I will grant you admittance with one companion.

He made a wee opening for them, and they entered. Then he closed the circle once more.

The demon king said to the old sage, How is it you have come to settle in my domain?

The old sage replied, Why is it your domain? It is my domain.

The king asked, Are you not afraid of me?

The old sage answered, No.

The king repeated, You are not afraid? He then stretched himself out and expanded to an exceedingly large size, towering up to the sky, and looked as if he were going to swallow the old sage.

The sage responded, I have not the slightest fear of you. But, to be quite honest, you should be afraid of me.

So he went and prayed for a bit. Great clouds billowed and thunder boomed. The thunderclaps massacred all the royal demon ministers, leaving only the demon king and his companion. The king begged the old sage to stop the thunderclaps, and he stopped them.

The king said to the old sage, As you are such a powerful person, I shall gift you with a book of all the demon genealogies.

There are wonder workers who may know a single demon's lineage, but they do not know the lines of all the demons. I will give you a book containing every demon's lineage, for they are all registered in it for the king, even the ones just born.

The king dispatched his companion to fetch the book. (It turns out it was a felicitous decision for the old sage to let the demon king bring a companion, otherwise whom would he have sent for the book?) The book was brought, and the old sage opened it and saw described there the myriads and multitudes of demon families. The king told the sage that the demons would never harm his family and ordered the sage to bring him portraits of all the members of his family. And whenever a child was born, its portrait was immediately to be brought to the king to ensure that no harm would come to any member of the old sage's family.

Later, when the time came for the old sage to depart this world, he called his children together and left them his will, telling them, I entrust this book to you. You have surely seen that I could have used this book for the sake of goodness. Yet, I never did. For I have put my trust in Blessed God, so neither shall you use the demons' book. Even if there should be one among you who could use it for goodness' sake, let him not do so. He should only have faith in Blessed God.

Thereupon the sage died, and the book became an heirloom and came into the possession of his grandson, who also had the power to use it. But he, too, had faith in Blessed God and did not use it, as the old sage had commanded in his will.

The talebearers among the demons tried to inveigle the old sage's grandson, Since you have marriageable daughters but nothing with which to support them and marry them off, you should use the book.

The sage's grandson did not know it was demons tempting him, believing these thoughts had come from his own heart. So he travelled to his grandfather's grave and asked him, In your will you commanded us never to use the demons' book but only to have faith in Blessed God. Now, however, my heart is prompting me to use it.

From beyond the grave his grandfather replied, Even though you might use it for good, it is better simply to have faith in Blessed God and never use it. Blessed God will help you.

And this the grandson did.

And it came to pass...

The king of the country where the sage's grandson now lived took ill. He consulted physicians, and they were unable to find a cure. Owing to a heatwave that had struck the country, medicines were of no use. So the king decreed that all the Jews should pray for him.

Our demon king, the cloud went on, said that since the old man's grandson had the power to use the book for good, but he did not do so, we ought to do him a kindness.

He ordered me to become a cloud to put an end to the heatwave so that that country's king might be cured by the medicines he already took as well as by those he had yet to take. The grandson knew nothing of all this. It was for this reason I became a cloud.

The cloud was brought before the demon king. The demon king ordered that he return the strength that he received, which

39

had been taken from the king who built his palace on the isle in the sea. His strength was returned, and the son of the demon couple was released from his captivity and returned home.

The son, however, had suffered greatly, sapped of all strength by his torture. He harboured bitter resentment against the king's sorcerer who had captured him and caused him so much suffering. So he ordered his children and all his family forever to stalk that sorcerer.

However, among the demons there were talebearers who warned the sorcerer that there were demons lying in wait for him and that he should be on his guard. The sorcerer devised cunning schemes and called on other sorcerers who knew demon lineages beside the single one he knew so he could be protected from them as well. The son and his family bore the talebearers a deep grudge for having divulged their cunning plan to the sorcerer.

Once it happened that members of the son's family and some of the talebearers chanced to meet together near the demon king's watchtower. The son's family denounced the talebearers and, on account of their denunciation, the king executed the talebearers. The rest of the talebearers were deeply aggrieved about this and went and fomented a rebellion among the various demon tribes.

The demons were then beset by famine and frailty, violence and pestilence as wars were waged between the demon kings. As a result, there was an earthquake that caused all the earthworks to collapse completely and allowed the tree to be fully watered. All of the demons were obliterated and none were left.

Amen

FOURTH TALE

Of a King who Decreed the Conversion of the Jews

O NCE THERE WAS a king who ordered an expulsion of those in the land who would not convert to his faith. All who stayed in the country were forced to be baptized, and those who did not were expelled. There were those who relinquished all of their wealth and belongings and they left the country in poverty in order to stay true to their faith and remain Jews. And there were also some who were concerned for their personal wealth and well-being who stayed, and they became forced converts, who carried on their religion in secret but never dared to behave as Jews in public.

Later, that king died and his son became king. The new king took to the power of the throne zealously. He conquered many countries and demonstrated great skill. And after vigor-ously wresting control from the ministers of state, a group of ministers conspired to attack and murder him along with all of his children. Among the ministers was one who was a forced convert. He thought, I converted because I so deplored having to abandon all my goodly possessions and wealth. But now the king will be killed and the whole country will go to ruin without a ruler. Everyone will devour each other alive, because a country cannot be left without a ruler.

So he decided to go and inform the king without the others knowing. He went and revealed the assassination plot to the king. The king went to investigate the truth of the matter and, to this end, he dispatched guards on the night the attack was due to take place. All the conspirators were caught, and each was tried and convicted.

The king spoke to the minister who was a forced convert, and asked, What kind of an honour shall I bestow upon you for having saved my life and the lives of my children? Do I elevate you to the nobility? But you are already a minister of state. Do I give you money? But you have a fortune of your own. So, tell me, what kind of honour would you like? Whatever you wish, I will surely grant.

The convert responded, But will you really do as I ask?

The king said, Yes, I will surely grant whatever you wish.

The convert said, Swear on your crown and on your kingdom.

The king so swore.

Then the forced convert spoke, The only honour I seek is the privilege of being a Jew in public and to be able to wear my religious garments—my tallis and tefillin—as before, for all to see.

This vexed the king greatly, since Jews had been forbidden throughout his realm. Yet, he had no choice since he had sworn an oath that he would do whatever he was asked. The next morning the forced convert went and donned his woollen prayer shawl and leather prayer boxes and straps in public.

Later this king died and his son became king. The son began to rule the country with kindness, because he saw how people wanted a real change from the harsh rule of his father. He continued to expand the realm and was even more skilful. The king ordered all the seers of stars to assemble and he asked them, What could cause my royal line to be brought to an end? For he wished to protect it. The seers of stars told him that his line would not be brought to an end if he could protect himself from a bull and a sheep. This prophecy was recorded in the royal chronicles. The king cautioned his children to lead the country as he had, with kindness, and then he died.

Afterwards, his son became king and took to ruling the country with the zeal of his grandfather. He conquered even more territory and then, by a stroke of brilliance, it occurred to him: he issued a decree that nowhere in his domain should there be any cattle or sheep. That way the royal line would never be brought to an end. Thereafter, he had no fear of anything at all. He led the country with great skill and became a very great sage.

Then this king had another stroke of brilliance: he would conquer the entire world without firing a shot. For the earth is divided into seven continents. And there are seven celestial orbs—the Sun, the Moon, Mars, Mercury, Jupiter, Venus and Saturn—each associated with its own day of the week. Every orb shines its light on each of the continents. There are also seven types of metal—gold, silver, iron, quicksilver, tin, copper and lead—and each of the seven orbs holds dominion over its own unique metal.

The king set out to collect each of the seven kinds of metal. Then he ordered that all the gilded portraits of all the kings hanging in their palaces be brought to him. From all of these he composed the figure of a man. The man's head was made of

43

gold, his body of silver, and all of the other limbs were forged from the rest of the seven types of metal. He set this effigy of a man on a high mountain, and all the seven celestial orbs infused it with their light.

If anyone needed advice or counsel on what to do or what not to do, he could come to the figure and ask the particular limb whose metal came from the continent relating to the subject of his question. And were one to inquire whether to do a particular thing, if the answer were positive the limb would light up and glow. If negative, the limb would stay dark. Thus the king did. As a result, he conquered the entire world and amassed a tremendous fortune.

But the man of seven metals alone could not accomplish all the king wished for. Only when the king had cast down the arrogant and exalted the lowly would he have, at last, conquered the whole world. So the king issued edicts to all his generals and ministers, all those who held noble offices and titles, and he demoted them and stripped them of their rank—even those who had been appointed by his forebears and had served loyally. He deposed them all, and in their place he elevated low-born people, installing them in place of the nobility and ministers he had banished.

When the former forced convert was brought before the king and asked what his royal privilege was, he answered, My only privilege is that I am allowed to be a Jew in public on account of the favour I once did your grandfather. But the king stripped him of this privilege, and he was once more forced to hide his faith.

One night, the king lay down to sleep. In his dream, he saw a crystal-clear sky in which he could make out all the twelve signs of the zodiac, arrayed before him according to their time of year. And there he saw the stars forming Aries for the early spring month Nissan, which appeared as a wee lamb, and those of the following sign, Taurus, for the month of Iyyar. And he saw that this bull and this ram were mocking him. He awoke in great anger and was terribly frightened. He ordered that the royal chronicles be brought to him, and there he recalled what was recorded: that only by the bull and the sheep would his royal line come to an end. He was seized with a terrible dread. So he told the queen and his dread spread to her and then to their children, until they could not contain the terrible fear in their hearts. They summoned a host of oneiromancers to interpret the dream and propose a solution. Yet he turned a deaf ear to them and was consumed by his terrible fear.

A sage came to him and said that he had received a teaching from his father that the sun emits 365 rays, and the place where all of them converge shines bright. An iron rod emerges from this spot, and all who are afraid may come there and be relieved of their fear. The king took well to this teaching.

So he headed out with his wife and his children and the entire royal family to this very place. And the sage came with them. On the road stood an angel of wrath. They asked the angel the way, for there were many paths that branched off: a smooth path, a path filled with muck, a path full of holes, and other paths as well, including one that was four miles of all-consuming fire. The angel pointed them towards the path of fire and they

45

all began walking. The sage kept on guard for the fire that his father had cautioned would be there. Then he caught sight of the fire and saw how kings and Jews were walking about in the fire, each wearing a wool-fringed tallis and leather tefillin. The sage said to the king, I received a teaching that the four miles of fire ahead are all-consuming and I shall go no further. Do as you will, and if you wish to go, go.

The king thought for a moment. He saw how other kings were going about unharmed in the fire so surely he would be able to go through the fire, too. The sage said, My father taught that one cannot do so. But do as you will, and if you wish to go, go.

So the king, along with the entire royal family, headed into the fire, and they were all consumed in great agony.

When the sage returned home, the ministers of state were astonished that the king and the entire royal family had been destroyed. After all, he had protected himself from the bull and the sheep, so how could it be that he and his entire line had been wiped out?

The forced convert then spoke up: It is because of me that he has been extirpated. The seers of the stars had prophesied it all, but they simply did not understand what they had seen. For it is from the bull's hide that the leather boxes and straps of the tefillin are made. And from the sheep comes the wool that fringes the tallis. And it is owing to them that the king and his entire line were cut off. For kings that allow Jews to live freely in their lands, who allow them to wear their tallis and tefillin, such kings may walk the path of fire and come to no harm. But the king who allows no Jews to wear their garments of prayer or to live freely in his country, he and his entire line will be wiped off the earth. This is why the zodiacal bull and ram scorned him. Indeed the seers of the stars saw that the destruction of his reign would be on account of the bull and the ram, but they did not understand what they had seen or how it would truly be the end of the line of the king.

Amen
And so may all your
enemies perish,
O Lord

FIFTH TALE

Of a Prince of Jewels

O NCE THERE WAS a king and the king had no children. He went and consulted with doctors to ensure that his kingdom would not pass into the hands of others. However, no physician could help him.

So he decreed that all of the Jews should pray for him to have an heir. The Jews sought a tzaddik who could pray most effectually for the king to have children. They searched and searched until they found a hidden tzaddik, and they asked him to pray for the king to have a child. The tzaddik replied that he was ignorant of such things. The king was informed about this supposedly ignorant hidden tzaddik and he issued a summons.

The tzaddik was brought before the king, and the king said to him kindly, You must know that the Jews here are under my authority and I can do with them what I will. So I kindly ask you to pray that I might have children.

The tzaddik promised that in one year's time the king would, indeed, have a child. Then he went home.

The queen gave birth to a daughter, and the princess showed signs of greatness. By the time she was four years old, she had accrued tremendous wisdom and spoke every language and could play musical instruments. Kings came from every land to see her, and this filled her father, the king, with great joy.

But the king still very much wanted to have a son so that the kingdom would not pass into others' hands. So he again decreed that the Jews should pray that he might have a son. They, in turn, searched for the earlier tzaddik but they could not find him, for he had already died. So they kept looking until they discovered another hidden tzaddik. They told him that he needed to give the king a son. The tzaddik replied that he was ignorant of such things. The king was again informed and he told this tzaddik what he had told the previous one about the Jews being under his authority and the like. The wise tzaddik said, But will you be able to do as I instruct?

The king replied, Yes.

The tzaddik told him, I need you to bring me all kinds of jewels, each with its own unique quality (for kings maintain an inventory in which all kinds of precious stones are recorded).

The king replied, I would give away half of my kingdom if only I could have a son.

He went and gathered a variety of jewels, which the tzaddik took. He ground them down and poured the pulverized precious stones into a goblet filled with wine. He gave half the goblet of wine to the king to drink and the other half to the queen. Then he assured them that they would have a son who would be made of jewels and he would have the unique qualities of each of the gems. Then he went home.

The queen gave birth to a son and the king was filled with joy. The son, however, was not made of precious jewels. But by the time he was four years old, he was showing signs of greatness—more gifted than all other sages, and he could speak in all the languages of the world. Kings came from far and wide to see him.

The princess saw that she was no longer as important and she grew jealous of her brother. Her only consolation was that the tzaddik's promise that the child would be made entirely of jewels was false. At least, that did not seem to be the case.

Once the prince was chopping wood and he cut his finger. The princess ran over to bandage him and there, in the wound, she saw a jewel. She was so overcome with jealousy that she became sick. Several physicians came to attend her, but they could find no cure. So sorcerers were summoned, and among them was a sorcerer in whom she confided the truth of how she had become ill on account of her brother. She asked the sorcerer if it were possible that there was some sort of magic that might turn a person into a leper.

The sorcerer replied, Yes.

So she asked the sorcerer, But could not another sorcerer be found who could undo that sorcery and heal him?

The sorcerer told her, If the magic charm is thrown into water, it can never be undone.

All this she contrived and cast the charm into water. And the prince became terribly afflicted with leprosy, with lesions on his nose and face and all over his body. The king went and consulted with doctors and sorcerers. But none could help him.

So the king decreed that the Jews should pray for him. The Jews went in search of the tzaddik who had promised the king a son. He was found and, as he was being brought to the king, the tzaddik prayed constantly to Blessed God, for he had assured the king that his son would be made of jewels and this had not been fulfilled. He argued with the Almighty, Did I make such a promise for my own glory? I did this for Your glory alone. And yet, it did not come to pass as promised.

The tzaddik came to the king and he prayed that the prince's leprosy be healed. But to no avail. Then he realized that there was sorcery at work. But this tzaddik was greater than any sorcerer. The tzaddik went and informed the king about the sorcery and the magic charm, which had been cast into water. The prince could not be healed unless the source of the charm were likewise thrown into water.

The king said, I shall give you all the sorcerers in the world to throw into the water so long as my son is cured.

The princess took fright and ran to the water to retrieve the charm. But she did not know where it lay and fell into the depths.

There was a terrible outcry when the princess sank into the water. But the tzaddik came and announced that now the prince would be healed.

And healed he was. All his sores dried up and fell off. Then the skin sloughed off his whole body and, indeed, all could see that he was made entirely of jewels and had the unique qualities of each precious stone, just as the tzaddik had promised.

SIXTH TALE

Of a Humble King's Portrait

A story:

ONCE THERE WAS a king who had a sage. The king said to his sage, There is a king whose seal indicates that he is both a mighty and valiant warrior and also a man of truth and humility. With regard to his might and valour, I know that to be the case. For the sea surrounds his domain, and on the sea sails his navy armed with cannon, allowing no one to land. Further inland from the sea the country is girt by a large swamp. Through this swamp there is but one lone path, wide enough for a single person to pass, and defended by more cannon. Were any to come to wage war, the cannon would fire on them. Thus none can reach his domain.

But as for his being a man of truth and humility, the king went on, that I cannot say. I want you to bring me his portrait.

The king, you see, had a royal portrait collection. But no king possessed the portrait of the island king, because that king kept himself hidden from people, seated behind a curtain, and distant from his subjects.

The sage then went forth into that country and decided he needed to understand its ways. How might he come to understand such things? Through its jokes. Because if one needs to understand a thing's essence, one has to get a feel for the jokes about it.

There are, of course, many kinds of jokes. If, say, someone were to wish to cut another person to the quick with his words but the object of his barb then took offence, he might add, I am only joking, as the Good Book says: As a mad man who casteth firebrands and arrows and saith, Am not I in sport? And sometimes someone really does mean it only as a joke, but his words still hurt the other person. So clearly there are various kinds of jokes.

Now there is a country that is the epitome of all the countries in the world.

And in that country is a city that is the epitome of all the cities in the country that is the epitome of all countries.

There is a house that is the epitome of all the houses in that city, the city that is the epitome of all cities in the country that is the epitome of all counties.

In this house can be found a man who is the epitome of all householders, in this house that is the epitome of all houses in the epitome of all cities, in the epitome of all countries.

And that man makes the jests and jokes of the entire country.

Now, the sage had brought with him a lot of money when he came to the country. There he saw all the kinds of derision and joking that went on, and he understood from them that the country was full of deception. He watched their mockery and how they deceived one another in business. And when one of them sought recourse in city hall, lies were told and bribes were taken. So one appealed to a higher court, but there was more lying, and everyone made a jesting mockery of this perversion of justice.

The sage came to understand from all this mockery that the country was full of lies and deception and there was no truth there. So he went and did business in the country and let himself be duped. He sought recourse in court, where lies and bribery abounded. So he paid a bribe. But the very next day, all that had transpired was forgotten, so he appealed to a higher court. That court, too, was full of lies. And so this went on until he reached the county's Senate, which was also fraught with fraud and bribery. So it was until he reached the court of the king himself.

When he appeared before the king he said, Over whom are you king? Your country is overrun with lies, from start to finish. There is no truth in it whatsoever. He then began to detail the duplicity of the country.

As he listened to what the sage had to say, the king inclined his ear towards the curtain to hear better, because it was an immense surprise to encounter a man who was so aware of his country's duplicity. The royal ministers, too, listened to what he had to say and grew increasingly vexed. But the sage kept recounting the country's duplicity. The sage concluded, One could say that you, O king, are very much like the rest of your realm, hiding your face as you benefit from deception just like the rest of your subjects. On the other hand, one might equally infer that you are a man of truth and therefore unlike the rest, and that you hide away because you cannot bear to see your country's deceitfulness.

He then started heaping praise upon the king. For the king was a very humble man, and, as our sages of old taught, *Wherever you find His might and valour, there you shall find His humility*. For this is the way of a truly humble man: the more he is praised and lauded, the smaller he becomes in his own estimation and grows humbler still. As the sage kept praising and lauding him, the king's humility increased and he grew smaller and smaller until he had become nothing. Unable to contain himself, the king threw back the curtain so he could lay eyes on the sage, demanding, Who is he that knows and understands all these things?

The face of the king was thereby revealed. The sage gazed upon it and went on to paint the king's portrait, which he brought to his own king.

SEVENTH TALE

Of a King's Journey

*I will tell you
of a journey I took.*

A story:

ONCE THERE WAS a king who had been engaged in several difficult wars. These he won and took numerous prisoners.

*Perhaps I shall tell you the whole story,
so that you might understand.*

Every year the king held a great banquet on the anniversary of his victory. The grand fete was attended by all the royal ministers and noblemen, as is the way of kings. Burlesques were staged that poked fun at all the nations, Turks and others alike. They parodied the customs and behaviours of every nation, and, no doubt, mocked the Jews as well.

The king ordered that he be brought a book he remembered, wherein each nation's customs and behaviours were recorded. Whatever page he opened the book to, he saw that each lampooned nation was described in precisely the same way as on the page. Clearly the one who planned the burlesque had also read this very book.

As the king was perusing the book he noticed a spider crawling along the edges of the pages and a fly standing on the page itself. Where would the spider go? Obviously, towards the fly. But just as the spider had crept up to the fly, a wind came and riffled that page of the book, preventing the spider from reaching the fly. So it retreated. But the spider was only pretending to withdraw in order to give the appearance of not wanting to get at the fly. Then, when the page had settled back in place, the spider once again tried to approach the fly, and once again the page was riffled, keeping the spider from the fly. So it retreated once more. This happened several times. The next time the spider approached the fly, it crept along until it could reach one of its legs across and secure the page. This time, when the wind riffled the page, the spider was already partially on it. And when the page settled back in place, the spider remained between the pages, and there it crept along, precariously underneath, until it was completely hidden away.

As for the fly, I shall not tell you what became of it.

The king observed all of this and was quite fascinated. He understood that this was no trifle, and that something important was being shown to him. All the royal ministers had noticed the king's rapt attention and astonishment. As for the king, he began to ponder what it all meant and he dozed off ruminating on the book.

He dreamt that he was holding a precious crystal. He gazed into it and saw hordes of people coming out of it. So he threw the crystal down. Now, it was customary for the portraits of the kings to be hung above their thrones and for their crowns to be suspended above. In his dream the king saw the people who had come out of the crystal were now taking down his portrait and ripping off its head. Then they took his crown and flung it into the mud. They then ran at him intending to kill him, but a page from the book he had fallen asleep on riffled up and shielded him. The people could do nothing to him so they withdrew. Then the page settled back in place. Once again the people tried to kill him, and once again the page rose and shielded him. This happened several times.

The king was very curious to see which page it was that was protecting him, what customs were recorded on it, and which nation was described there. But he was afraid to take his eyes off his assailants and started yelling, Help! Help!

All the royal ministers who were seated there heard him yelling in his sleep and wanted to wake him up. But there was no courteous way to awaken a king directly, so instead they banged on various objects to rouse him. But still he did not stir.

Just then, a tall mountain came to the king and asked, Why are you yelling? I have been asleep for such a long time and no one has ever woken me up, but now you have gone and done so.

The king said to him, Why should I not yell when there are people rising against me and trying to kill me and I have only this page to shield me?

The mountain replied, If that page is shielding you, then you need fear nothing. For many enemies are risen up against me with only this same page shielding me. Come, I will show you.

The mountain pointed out the myriads and multitudes of people that had set themselves against it in encampments round about. All of them are feasting and making merry, the mountain went on, playing music and dancing. They rejoice whenever one of their rank has devised a clever new stratagem to conquer me. And so it is at each encampment. But that page of the book of customs that shields you also shields me.

At the summit of the mountain was a signpost. Upon it was inscribed both the customs from the shielding page as well as which nation they belonged to. But since the mountain was so tall, the writing could not be made out. But down below there was another signpost upon which it was inscribed that whosoever had all his teeth could reach the mountaintop. Blessed God had granted that grass should grow to form a path where the mountain was to be climbed. But whosoever trod there, lost all his teeth. No matter whether he had come on foot, or had ridden a horse, or had driven a cart pulled by oxen—all his teeth fell out. The king saw there were great mountainous heaps of white teeth.

Then the people from the crystal took the king's portrait and put it back together; and they took his crown and washed it off and hung it back up in place.

Then the king awoke.

Right away he looked for the page that had shielded him to find out which nation's customs were written on it. There he found the customs of the Jews. He began looking at the page that contained the Truth and he understood its rightful way. He decided that he must assuredly become a Jew. But what could he do to put the world on the path of right and bring all to the truth? He decided he would set out to find a sage who could precisely interpret his dream. He took two companions and he travelled the world with them, not as a king but as a commoner.

He travelled from one city to another, asking, Where might one find a sage who can interpret dreams precisely?

He was told of a place where such a sage could be found. So he travelled there and found him. He told the sage the truth: that he was a king, that he had been victorious in war, and the whole story from beginning to end. Then he asked the sage to interpret his dream.

The sage replied, I cannot interpret your dream myself. But there is a certain day in a certain month when I gather all the fragrant herbs I need to make an incense and grind them into a compound. Then I burn the incense and allow the smoke to settle over the seeker. Then he may envision what he wishes to see and wants to know. And all is revealed.

The king decided that since he had devoted so much time to this endeavour already, he would wait until the month and day the sage had mentioned. When that day arrived, the sage did as he had described and the king was enveloped by the smoke of the incense.

Then he began to see everything, even what had happened to him before he was born when his soul was still in the heavenly realms. He saw his soul being led through all the worlds to be tested on his way to this world. A voice bellowed, Whosoever has a charge with which to indict this soul, let him come forward! But there was no one with such an indictment.

Just then someone came running up, yelling, Almighty God! Hear my plea! If this soul should be allowed to enter the world, what will I do? What is it You created me for?

It was the Adversary—the Satan—to whose yelling boomed

the reply, This soul must go down into the world. And as for you, Adversary, be reconciled to it.

Then the Satan took his leave, and the king's soul was led further through more worlds until at last it was brought to the Heavenly Tribunal to be adjudged whether it was fit to descend into this world. The Tribunal awaited the Adversary, who had not yet appeared. A messenger was dispatched to summon him so the trial could get underway. When he at last arrived, he brought with him a stooped old man, a greybeard he appeared to know from long, long ago. Grinning, the Adversary said, I am reconciled to it. This soul may go down into the world.

The king's soul was permitted to leave and descend into this world. Then the king saw what had happened to him from the start of his earthly life until its end, and how he had become a king, and the wars he had fought, and the prisoners he had taken. Among those prisoners there had been a comely woman who possessed all manner of worldly grace, which came not from her alone, but from a jewel she wore. It was by means of this jewel that she radiated such grace and such charm.

Now the mountain is forbidden to be climbed by anyone except sages and the illustrious.

He did not recount any further.

There was more to this tale,
including the matter of the prisoners,
but I failed to record it all properly.

EIGHTH TALE

Of a Rabbi and his Only Son

A story:

ONCE THERE WAS a rabbi and the rabbi had no children. Later, he had a son and the rabbi raised this only child of his and prepared him for marriage. The rabbi's son would sit in the garret of the house, studying the holy books, as is the custom among illustrious families. There he could be found, continuously engaged in study and prayer. The rabbi's only son was so skilful that he performed a worthy deed that allowed him to attain the brilliance of the moon, the lesser luminary of the universe.

Still, he carried with him a sense of emptiness whose cause he did not know. Learning and praying held no appeal for him. He opened up to two of his young friends and they advised him to go and travel to a certain tzaddik.

The son went to tell his father about how his service to God and his devotion to study held no appeal for him, that he felt something was lacking but did not know what. For this reason, he wished to travel to the tzaddik that his friends had suggested. His father replied, Why would you ever want to go to such riff-raff when you are more learned than he is and come from a far better family? It would be unseemly for you to go to him, so lay off this path.

The father thus prevented his son from going to see the tzaddik, and the rabbi's only son returned to his studies. Yet he still felt the same sense of emptiness as before. He again sought the advice of others and again they counselled him to travel to that particular tzaddik. So he returned to his father, who, yet again, dissuaded him and would not allow him to go. This happened several more times. The rabbi's only son kept feeling that he was lacking and he longed to fill the void in him, even though he did not know how. Once more, he went to his father and earnestly pleaded with him until, at last, his father relented and allowed him to go. His father did not wish to let his son travel alone, however, since he was his one and only child.

The father said, Now look, I shall travel with you and then I will show you that this tzaddik is a worthless nobody. They harnessed the wagon and headed off. The father continued, Now I shall set this as a test. If things go according to plan, it is a sign that this was meant to be. But if they do not, we were not meant to make this journey and we will head back.

So off they went. As they were travelling, they came to a small bridge. One horse slipped and fell. The wagon was overturned and they all nearly drowned. The father declared, You see, things are not going to plan at all! This journey is not meant to be. So they headed home.

The rabbi's only son returned once more to his studies and again felt something lacking. But he did not know what it was. He exhorted his father once more, and his father once more was obliged to join his son on the journey to the tzaddik. As they went, the father again declared this to be a test and, as before, they would see if everything went according to plan. On the road, both of the wagon's axles suddenly broke. The father said, You see, our travelling is not meant to be. Is it an everyday occurrence that both axles just happen to break? This wagon has travelled many times and never before has such a thing happened. So they headed home again.

The rabbi's only son once more resumed his studies and, again, felt that same lack as before. His young companions kept pressing him to journey to the tzaddik. So the son went back to his father and implored him, as before, to allow him to travel. The son said, But we shall not set a test this time. Indeed, horses slipping and axles breaking are everyday occurrences. Such things are not in the least extraordinary.

So they set out and arrived at an inn to spend the night. There they met a merchant who struck up a conversation with them, as is the way of travelling merchants. But they did not tell him that they were travelling to the tzaddik, since the rabbi was ashamed to be on a journey to a so-called saint. Instead, they spoke of worldly affairs until the conversation turned to the subject of the tzaddikim of the Hasidim and where these were to be found. The merchant told them about the tzaddikim in one place after another. So they began to tell the merchant about the one they were travelling to see. The merchant replied in a surprising manner that this was no respectable saint but rather an impious rogue. I am returning from visiting him now, the merchant said, and I was with him when he committed an outright sin.

65

The father exclaimed to his son, You see, my child, how plainly he states it! How this merchant disparages the tzaddik! And he has just come from him. So the rabbi and his only son headed home.

Thereupon the son died and came to his father in a dream. The father saw his son yelling in a rage, and he asked him, Why are you so angry?

The son answered that he should go to the holy tzaddik they had intended to visit and the tzaddik would explain why he was so angry.

The rabbi awoke and thought that this was simply a dream and that it was of no significance. Then he dreamt the same thing again. And, yet again, he thought that this was just a fancy of his imagination. But when he dreamt it a third time, he understood that this was no trifle. So he set off to visit the tzaddik.

On the way, he came across the merchant he had met before when he was travelling with his son. The rabbi recognized him and said, You are the one I saw at the inn.

He answered, Indubitably I am. Then he yawned his mouth wide and said, Now, if you wish, I shall devour you.

The rabbi replied, What are you talking about?

He responded, Remember when you were travelling with your son and first the horse slipped on the bridge? Then, the wagon's axles broke? And then you met me and I told you that the tzaddik was a rogue? Now that I have rid you of your son, you may travel on to the tzaddik. For your son had attained the brilliance of the lesser luminary, and the holy saint he wished to visit has the brilliance of the sun, the foremost luminary of the universe. If the two of them were to have joined together, the Messiah would have come. But now I have rid you of him and you may go…

Then, in the midst of speaking, the merchant suddenly vanished, leaving the rabbi by himself with no one to respond to.

The rabbi travelled on to the tzaddik, crying: Help me, Help me! Woe to those who are gone and are never to be found!

May Blessed God save us from
our inclination towards evil
and return us to the
rightful truth.
Amen

NINTH TALE

Of a Wise Man and a Simpleton

A story:

O NCE THERE WERE two burghers who lived in the same city. They were both exceptionally wealthy and had large houses. Each burgher had one son, and they went to school together. One son was very clever and the other simple—not an idiot by any means, just rather foolish. The two boys loved one another very much. It was no matter that one was so clever and intelligent and the other simple-hearted and silly; they loved each other nonetheless.

As time went on, both burghers met with a reversal of fortunes and their status declined until they had lost nearly everything. They were left destitute, with their houses as their sole possession. The sons were grown by then, and the burghers told their children, We can no longer afford to support you. Do what you can to earn your keep.

The foolish son went off to become a shoemaker.

Given his intelligence, the clever son did not want to take on a simple trade. He decided that he would head into the world to see what he could do. While walking around the market square, he saw a large carriage pass by, drawn by four leather-harnessed horses. He asked the merchants riding in it, Where do you come from?

They answered, From Warsaw.

And where are you going now?

Back to Warsaw, they responded.

Perhaps you might need an apprentice? he asked them.

The merchants saw that he was clearly a bright young man and quite industrious, and they took a liking to him. So they took him along. They travelled together and earned quite a sum on their way.

When he arrived in Warsaw, since he was a deep thinker, he reasoned, Now that I am already here in Warsaw, why should I remain apprenticed to these merchants? Perhaps there is a better place for me than with them. I shall go look and see where such a place might be. He went to the market square, where he began making inquiries, asking about the merchants who had brought him to Warsaw and whether he might be better suited to a position with others. He was told that the merchants were upstanding people and he would do well to stay; but, on the other hand, it might also be difficult, since they had business dealings so far and wide.

As he was walking, he saw some shop boys also going about in the market square. They were bustling about, as shop boys do, in their unique fashion with their caps and pointed shoes and their charming demeanour and fancy dress. Since he was such a deep thinker and clever young man this all appealed to him, for it seemed to be a very fine occupation and was in one fixed location that he could call home. So he went to the merchants who had brought him to the city and he thanked them and told them that it did not seem ideal for him to stay on and that he had already paid his fare for the journey by what he had earned for them on the way. He took his leave of them and arranged to be taken on by a Warsaw shopkeeper.

According to the custom of shop boys, one must first be an underling and do the heavy lifting in exchange for little pay. Afterwards, one is promoted to shop boy. Thus the shopkeeper doled out the heavy labour to him and routinely dispatched him to carry merchandise to nobles, as is the way of the shop underlings, whose task it is to lug bolts of cloth in the crooks of their arms. The work was very hard for him. Once he had to deliver merchandise to the upper storey of a building, which was especially difficult. So he began to ruminate, as is the way of deep thinkers, What good does this work do me? The point of such a livelihood is that it allows one to get married and be a breadwinner. But I do not need to think about that now; there is time for all that later. For now, it would be better if I travelled the world and visited many lands.

He went to the market square and saw some merchants riding in a large carriage. He asked them, Where are you going?

They answered, To Leghorn.

Would you take me with you? he asked.

Yes, they replied. So they brought him along, travelling from Warsaw to Italy. And from Italy he headed off to Spain.

Several years passed during his travels and he grew even cleverer as he spent time in many countries. He thought, Now I must seek a more practical purpose for myself. So he began to ruminate, in his philosophical way, on what he should do. The idea of learning goldsmithing appealed to him, for it is a fine trade and a lovely craft and it requires great wisdom. It is also a lucrative profession. As he was a deep thinker and exceptionally clever, it did not take him many years to learn his craft. He picked it up in one season alone and became a master artisan, an expert goldsmith, even better than the smith who had taught him.

Later, he started ruminating again in his philosophical manner, Even though I have mastered this craft, I am still unsatisfied by it. After all, one thing may be highly regarded today and then, later, it is something else.

So he set himself up with a gemcutter and, owing to his wisdom, he picked up this craft in the brief span of one season. Some time passed before he again began reflecting philosophically, Even though I have now mastered these two trades, who knows if either of them will continue to be as well regarded as they are now. It would be ideal for me to learn a trade that will always be highly esteemed.

He thought that with all of his cleverness and deep thinking he ought to study medicine, which is a field that is always needed and will be esteemed always. As is the custom when studying medicine, one must first learn Latin—both how to speak and write—and one must also study philosophy. Since he was so very clever, he learnt all of this in the brief span of one season and he became a great physician and philosopher, the sage of all sages.

But then, everything began to seem trivial, and the whole world appeared worthless to him. He felt as if there were no sense in anything at all. Owing to his cleverness he had become a great artisan and sage and doctor, and yet, to him, all was pointless. He decided he ought to find a purpose and to find a wife. He considered the idea, But if I were to marry here, who would even know what had become of me? I would rather return home so that they might all see what I have become. I left when I was only a lad and now I have achieved such greatness.

So he picked himself up and headed home. He was terribly miserable on the way. Because of his great wisdom there was no one he could talk to, and he felt no accommodations were suitable. And so he was always very miserable.

For the meantime, let us set aside the story of the clever son.
We shall now relate what became of the simple one.

The simple son learnt the craft of shoemaking. Since he was so simple, he had to study his trade a long while until he had got the hang of it, although, even then, not fully. He took a wife and earned a living by his trade. Yet since he was so simple and did not have a firm grasp of his craft, his earnings were terribly meagre. He hardly had time to eat because he always had to work, owing to his lack of expertise. As he worked, boring holes with his awl and passing waxed ends through the leather, he would take a bite of some bread and eat.

But his nature was to be merry always. He acted as if every new day was a cause for constant celebration and that he had every dish to eat, every beverage to drink and every garment to wear. He would call to his wife, Wife, bring me something to eat! She would bring him a crust of bread, which he would gobble up. Then he would say, Give me some barley soup! And

73

she would slice another piece of bread for him and he would gobble it up. Then he would heap praise on her, How fine and good this soup is! Then he would ask her to bring him some meat, and she would bring him yet another hunk of bread, which he gobbled up, lauding, How fine this meat is! And the same with any other dish he asked for. He would order a dish, and each time she would bring him a scrap of bread. And he would take delight in it all and compliment each dish's excellence as if he had really eaten it. Indeed, he genuinely felt as if the bread he ate had the taste of each of the delicious dishes he wished for. Given his levity and jollity, he savoured his bread as if it were every delicacy in the world.

He would say, Bring me some beer to drink, my wife! And she would bring him water, and he would praise how fine a beer it was. Then he would say, Bring me some mead. She would bring him water, which he praised, What delicious mead this is! Bring me wine or some liquor, he would say. Again she would bring him water and again he enjoyed it and praised the drink as he quaffed it.

The same was the case with his clothing. He and his wife possessed one old pelt between the two of them. If he needed to wear it to go to the market, he would say, My wife, give me my pelt. And she gave it to him. If he needed to wear a sheepskin coat for a more dignified occasion, he would say, My wife, bring me my sheepskin. And she would fetch the old pelt for him. He would delight in his coat and commend it, What a fine sheepskin coat this is! If he needed to put on a gaberdine to go to the prayer house, he would call to his wife and say, Wife, bring me my gaberdine!

When she brought the pelt, he would say, What an elegant and lovely gaberdine this is! The same when he needed to dress up in a waistcoat, she would bring him the pelt and again he would take great delight in it, exclaiming, What an elegant and lovely waistcoat this is! And it was much the same with everything else. He was always filled with joy and cheer and mirth.

When he completed a shoe, it might have three sides, since he really did not have much of a handle on his trade. But he would take the shoe into his hands and praise it and take great pleasure in it. He would say, My wife, what a lovely and fine little shoe this is! What a sweet and adorable and delightful little shoe!

She would ask, If that is the case, why do the other shoemakers earn three gulden for a pair and you only get half a thaler—a mere quarter of what they earn?

Why should I care, he replied. That is their business and this is mine. Why should we discuss other people's affairs? Let us better figure out how much profit I make on a shoe. The leather costs this much, the resin and wax ends cost that much, the lasts cost this much, and all the other materials that much. All in all, I net ten groschen, so why should I worry when I still make a profit? And so he was always nothing but cheerful and merry.

He was a source of ridicule for everybody else, however, and all the mockery they desired they got out of this source, for they had someone—an apparent nincompoop—to deride whenever they desired. People would come to converse with him for the express purpose of mocking him. The simple man would always respond, No fooling, right?

Straight away they would answer him, Absolutely! No fooling!

After inquiring in that way, he would chat with them. He did not want to keep guessing if all was meant in jest, for he really was quite simple. Yet, if he determined that someone was, indeed, pulling his leg, he would say, What does it matter if you are smarter than I am? You are still a fool. For what am I, after all? It is no great shakes to be wiser than a fool. Such was the way of this simple man.

Now, he resumes telling about the clever one:

Meanwhile, the clever son's return caused quite a stir in his hometown, as he was coming back with all his grandeur and brilliance. The simple man also ran to greet him with great joy, telling his wife, Bring me my waistcoat! I am going to meet my dear friend and see him after so long!

So she brought him the old pelt and he headed off to meet him. The clever son was riding grandly in a coach when the simple man met him and shouted his greetings to him with joy and great affection, How are you, my dear brother? Praise be to God who has brought you home and has granted me the privilege of seeing you again.

The clever one looked at him. Despite the whole world seeming worthless to him—and all the more so this man who looked like a lunatic—out of the deep love they held for each other from their youth, he embraced him. They rode into town together.

The two burghers, the fathers of the clever and simple sons, had died while the clever one was off in the world and had bequeathed their houses to their children. For his part, the simple

76

man had moved into his father's house, which was now his own. Since the clever one was abroad, no one had taken care of his house and it had gone to rack and ruin. Nothing at all was left of it. The clever son had no home to go to when he arrived, so he stopped at an inn. He was terribly miserable there since this was not the sort of inn he would have wanted.

Now the simple man had a new occupation. He would regularly head over to visit the clever one with affection and joy. Seeing how miserable he was at the inn, the simple man said to the clever man, My brother, come over to my house and stay with me. I will gather all of my things together and my home will be all yours.

This idea appealed to the clever one and he went over to stay with the simple man. But the clever man was always miserable. Since he had gained renown as a great sage and a great artisan and a great physician, a nobleman came to ask him to make a gold ring. So he made a very fine ring, engraved with intricate designs, including the figure of a tree which was truly a marvel. But when the nobleman came for it, he was displeased with the ring and the clever one was miserable about this. He knew that this ring with the engraving of the tree would have been esteemed in Spain and considered a masterpiece. Yet it was completely unappreciated here.

So it was another time, when a great nobleman came bringing a precious stone from a faraway land. He brought with him another gem that had a design engraved on it and he asked the clever one to engrave the same design onto the newly acquired stone. He then recreated the engraving, but his design was imperfect, although nobody could tell but him. When the nobleman came to collect his jewel, he was very pleased with the work. The clever one, however, was miserable about the flaw. He thought to himself, As clever as I am, it still happens that I make a blunder.

He was also brought to misery in his doctoring. Once he came to a patient and gave a cure that he well knew would allow this patient to survive; he would assuredly be healed by this cure since it was a most effective remedy. Then the patient died, and everyone said it was because of the clever man. He was terribly miserable about this. It also happened that he gave another patient a remedy, and when he got better, everyone said it was just a stroke of luck. This also made him most miserable. He was always afflicted with such misery.

Once he needed a garment. He went to see the tailor and took great pains to instruct him on how to make his garment according to the style he wished and was accustomed to. The tailor met all of the clever man's specifications for the garment but for the lapel, which was not to his liking. The clever man was quite miserable about this, too. He thought to himself, Even though no one notices it here, if I were to go out with such a lapel in Spain, I would be a laughing stock and derided for it. Thus he was continually made miserable.

The simple man frequently hastened to the clever one's side, bringing along his joy and cheer. He always found him in a wretched state, full of misery. He asked him, Why is it that, as brilliant and illustrious as you are, I am always merry and you are always so miserable? This struck the clever man as ironic, indeed, as he considered his friend mad. The simple one went on, Even when ordinary folks mock me, I know they are fools since, if they are only smarter than I am, they are still fools. All the more so when it comes to you. As clever as you are, what good does it do you to be smarter than me? Then he exclaimed, May the Almighty grant that you could only be more like me!

The clever man answered, It could very easily be that I become like you. For the Lord, Heaven forbid, might deprive me of my reason, or I might, Heaven forbid, become ill or take leave of my senses. For what are you, after all, but a nincompoop? But for you to become like me, to attain my level of brilliance, that is unquestionably impossible.

The simple man replied, With Blessed God all things are possible. In the blink of an eye, I could reach your level!

The clever one laughed and laughed.

The two sons came to be known as the wise man and the simpleton, and so they were called by all. Even though there are many clever and many simple people in the world, the bearers of these names were unmistakable to everyone in the city since the two had grown up there and had gone to school together. Yet one was extraordinarily brilliant and the other so very simple. In the official revision list, where the names of all men in the kingdom were recorded, the two were entered as Wiseman and Simpleton.

Once the king was reviewing the revision lists and he came across two entries where the surnames Wiseman and Simpleton were registered. The king was startled to see these names listed together and he wished to meet this twosome. The king recognized that if he were to summon them so unexpectedly they might be frightened. The one who was called Wiseman would not know how to respond, and this Simpleton might go mad from fear. So the king decided to dispatch a wise man to Wiseman and a simple man to Simpleton. But where does one find a simple person in the royal capital, a place where all are thought to be wise? Actually, the steward of the treasury is quite simple, for no one wishes to have a clever person in charge of the treasury. If he were too clever, he could use his wits to abscond with the country's fortune. For that reason, the treasury's steward was, indeed, quite a simpleton.

The king thus summoned a clever man and a simple man— the steward of the treasury—and dispatched them to Messrs Wiseman and Simpleton, with a letter in hand for each. He also sent a letter to the provincial governor, whose subjects included the two. The letter for the governor requested that he send his own correspondence in advance to Wiseman and Simpleton so that they would not be alarmed by the invitation. The governor ought to inform them that the royal request was not obligatory and that the king was not issuing a decree that they had to come to him, but rather it was up to them whether they wished to, since the king desired to meet them.

The royal delegates, wise and simple, journeyed out. They came to the provincial governor and delivered his letter. The governor made enquiries about the pair, and he was informed that Wiseman was an extraordinarily clever person and rather prosperous, and that Simpleton was utterly simple, a man who maintained that he wore all sorts of garments although he only possessed one single pelt. The governor considered this and decided it would be highly inappropriate for Simpleton to be brought before the king wearing this shabby old pelt. So he had clothing made for him that would be more appropriate and had those placed in the simple delegate's carriage to be delivered. He also sent along the missives the king had requested he write. Then the royal delegates rode off. When they arrived, they delivered all the letters. The clever delegate gave his to Wiseman and the simple one to Simpleton.

Upon receiving his letter, Simpleton called to the simple delegate who had brought it, and said, What could be in this letter, will you read it to me?

The delegate replied, I know by heart what the letter says: the king requests you come to him.

Simpleton shot back, No fooling?

That is the absolute truth, the delegate answered, no fooling.

Straightaway, Simpleton was filled with joy. He ran to his wife and said, My wife, the king has sent for me.

She replied, What on earth? Why has he sent for you?

He had no time to give an answer. He joyfully rushed right off and went and sat himself down in the carriage to travel with the royal delegate. There he saw the clothes that the governor had arranged, and he rejoiced even more that he had these clothes now and was very merry.

In the meantime, the king had learnt that the provincial governor was corrupt and he had him sacked. He considered that it might be good to have someone more humble as governor, a simple person. After all, a simple fellow would lead his land truthfully and honestly, since he would not be given to cunning or chicanery. The king thus ordered that Mr Simpleton, whom he had already sent for, be made governor. He issued a decree to that effect, ordering that when Simpleton got to the provincial capital he should be halted at the city gates and intercepted as soon as he arrived. Thereupon, he would be appointed to his position as governor. And so it was. His arrival was awaited at the city gates and, as soon as he passed through them, he was intercepted and told that he was now the provincial governor.

No fooling? he asked.

They answered, Of course not! No fooling at all.

And so he became the governor with all might and majesty.

Now the stars began to align for him and, as our Sages have taught, the right alignment of the stars brings wisdom. And with this change in his fortune, he gained some intelligence. He did not make use of this new wisdom, but rather conducted himself with the same simpleness as before. He ruled his province with simplicity and truth and honesty. There was no falsity about him, and he caused no grief to anyone. For one needs no great wit or intelligence to rule a land, only honesty and simplicity. If two people brought an issue before him to settle, he would determine, You are blameless, or, You are culpable. Thus he was always simple-hearted and honest, without falseness or deceit, and he ruled always with truth.

He was much loved throughout the province and had loyal councillors who truly loved him as well. Out of fondness for him, one of these councillors gave him some advice, Surely you must appear before the king, as he has already summoned you, and, moreover, it is the custom of all governors to report before the king. Now, even though you are so honest, and the king could not find in you any semblance of wrongdoing in your rule of the province, it is nevertheless the custom of the king that when he discusses matters, his conversation may stray to topics of philosophy or philology. So it would be well and courteous to reply to him in kind. Therefore it would be fitting for me to teach you philosophy and philology.

This pleased Simpleton. He thought, What is the harm in my learning philosophy and philology?

So he began studying and became adept in these subjects. At once he remembered what his friend Wiseman had said, how it was unquestionably impossible for him to reach his level of brilliance. But here I am, he thought, attaining it after all. Even though he acquired such wisdom, he never put it to use and continued ruling with his simplicity, just as before.

When he was summoned before the king, he was obligated to go and travel to him. First the king discussed how he was running his province. All this greatly pleased the king, for the king saw how he ruled with justice and truth and without any wrongdoing or deception. After this, the king began to discuss philosophy and philology, to which Simpleton responded accordingly. Now the king was even more pleased. The king said, I see that you are such a clever person and yet you rule with such simplicity.

The king was so very pleased with him that he made Simpleton a minister over all other ministers. He then ordered that he be given his own estate to settle in and that it be cloistered by very fine walls, as was only fitting. He also gave him a scroll naming him minister. And so it was—the cloister was finely built with very lovely walls in the place the king had ordered and there he ruled with might and majesty.

When the letter was delivered to Wiseman, he said to the wise man who had brought him the letter, Wait, spend the night here. We can talk things over and consider what to do.

That night he prepared a grand meal and, as they ate, Wiseman began to cogitate and contemplate in his wise and philosophical way. Then he spoke up and said, How comes it that the king should send for a commoner like me? Who am I that the king would summon me? What does it mean when he is such a mighty king, who possesses such a realm and such grandeur while I am so small in comparison? How can one make sense of such a thing as his summons? If I venture to say that it is on account of my wisdom, what does that amount to next to the king's? Does the king not have his own sages? And the king himself is certainly a great scholar, so why should he send for me? This all bewildered Wiseman greatly, and in his bewilderment he turned to the wise man who had delivered the letter, You know what I say? I am of the opinion that this indicates that there is really no king at all and that everyone is simply deluded into believing that there is one. Come now, how do you understand it? How does it add up that everyone allows themselves to be under the authority of one man that he should be their king? There is certainly no king at all.

The wise messenger answered, But I have brought you a letter from the king!

Wiseman countered, Did you take the letter directly from his hand?

No, he replied. Another man gave me the letter from the king.

So there you have it! Wiseman exclaimed. Now you see yourself that I am right and that there is no king at all. Just tell me this: you are from the royal city and were raised there, so tell me then, have you ever seen the king?

No, he replied.

Wiseman exclaimed, Now you see that I am right and that there really is no king in the world after all! For you, too, have never even laid eyes on him.

The royal delegate enquired in turn, If that is the case, who is ruling our country?

This I can explain clearly since I am well versed in such matters. I was in Italy where the custom is that there is a council of seventy men, and each man takes his turn ruling the country for a time. Then authority over the land passes from one councillor to the next.

Wiseman's words began to penetrate the other wise man's ears until both were convinced that there really was no king in the world at all. Then Wiseman said, Wait until morning, when I will prove there is certainly no king.

Wiseman woke up the next day and woke the wise delegate saying, Come outside with me and I will show you that the whole world is deceived and how it is that the king does not exist.

The two went to the market square, where they encountered a soldier and accosted him, asking, Who is it that you serve?

He answered, The king.

Have you ever in your life seen this king?

He answered, No.

At this Wiseman exclaimed, You see, it is just nonsense!

After this, they encountered an army officer and began to converse with him before asking, Whom do you serve?

The officer answered, The king.

Have you ever seen the king?

No.

There you have it! he announced. You see with your own eyes that they are all deceived and that there is no king at all.

Thus they were convinced that the king did not exist.

Wiseman said, Come, let us travel together and I will show you how everyone throughout the whole world is deceived into believing such utter nonsense.

The two headed off into the world, and everywhere they went they found everyone deceived. The nonexistence of the king became their prime example and they used the king as a criterion to assess just how deceived everyone was. If one held as true that there was a king, this was only confirmation of their having been duped. Just so, they gauged the world as they travelled on until they spent all that they had. First they had to sell one horse and then the other, until they sold all their possessions and were left travelling by foot, still assessing the whole world and finding everyone hoodwinked. So they became indigent vagabonds, lacking any esteem, as no one even took notice of these two paupers. Thus they continued to take stock of the world until they reached the city where Chief Minister Simpleton lived.

In that city lived a true wonder worker who was held in very high esteem because he did genuinely extraordinary things. He was renowned among the nobility and esteemed by them, too. When the two wise men came into the city and approached the wonder worker's home, they saw many wagons stopped there with sick people, a good forty or fifty of them. Wiseman assumed that a doctor lived there. He wanted to go inside to meet him since he was also a great doctor. He asked, Who lives here?

A wonder worker, he was told.

At this, he burst out laughing. Turning to his wise friend, he said, Yet again, more trickery and nonsense. This is even greater nonsense than the hoax about the king. Listen, brother, I will show you how this is all a deception and how everyone has been hoodwinked to believe such frauds.

Meanwhile, they had grown hungry and they had three or four groschen left between them. So they went to a public kitchen where one could order a meal for their three or four groschen. They ordered food and it was brought. As they were eating, they got to talking and ridiculing the fraud and deception of this wonder worker. The cook overheard them and got angry, since the wonder worker was highly regarded in town. He said to them, Finish your food and get out.

Then, one of the wonder worker's sons entered and the pair kept ridiculing the wonder worker in front of him. The cook berated them for mocking the wonder worker right in front of his son; he gave them a sound drubbing and kicked them out of the place.

Now the two were very angry. They wanted to bring charges against the one who had beaten them. They decided to go to the proprietor of the place where they had left their sacks to seek his advice on how to go about pressing charges against the cook at the public kitchen who had assaulted them. They went to the proprietor and told him all about the beating they had received at the hands of the cook. He asked them, What did he beat you for?

They told him that it was because they were talking about the wonder worker.

The owner replied, Of course it is not right that it should come to blows. But, in fact, you were wrong to speak so ill of the wonder worker, for he is very esteemed here.

The two saw that he, too, had been duped. They left him and found a local official. This official was a gentile. They told him the whole story about how they had been beaten and the official asked them, What did he beat you for?

Because we were talking about the wonder worker, they said.

Thereupon the official began doling out savage blows and kicked them out.

After they left him, they went to find a higher-ranking official who had more authority, but nothing led to any charges being brought. They went from one person to the next, each with a higher rank, until they found themselves outside the chief minister's palace where guards were stationed. The minister was informed that someone wished to see him and he ordered that he be allowed inside. So Wiseman came before the minister and as soon as he did, the minister recognized his old friend Wiseman immediately. Wiseman, however, did not recognize Simpleton because of his current grandeur. Right away, the minister began to speak to him, saying, Look how my simplicity has brought me to such grand heights and how low your wisdom has brought you.

At this Wiseman exclaimed, But you are my old friend Simpleton! We shall discuss all that later. At present, I am seeking a trial for an assault against me.

Simpleton asked him, Why were you beaten?

He answered, Because I was saying that the wonder worker was a fraud and a charlatan.

Simpleton the minister said to him, You continue to cling to your cleverness. Look, you once said that you could arrive at my level quite easily but that I could never attain yours. Now, behold, I have long ago attained your level and you still have not arrived at mine. I see that it is far more difficult to be simple.

However, since the minister knew him from long ago when he was once great, he ordered that clothing be made for him and asked that he be brought some food. While he was eating, they began chatting, and Wiseman started in with his idea about the nonexistence of the king. At this the minister Simpleton cried, What are you talking about?! I have seen the king myself!

Wiseman answered, laughing, But do you know for yourself that he was the king? Do you truly know it was he? Did you know his father or his grandfather and that they were kings, too? How do you know that this was really the king? Only because people told you it was! Just so have you been duped!

Simpleton grew very annoyed as he went on denying the existence of the king.

Just then, someone entered and announced, The Devil summons you.

Simpleton was startled by this and ran in terror to his wife. In a fright he told her how the Devil had summoned him. She advised him to go send for the wonder worker. So he did. The wonder worker came and gave him amulets and protective spells and told him that he had nothing to fear from now on. Simpleton had great faith in all of this.

Later, he was back at the table together with Wiseman, who asked, Why did you get so frightened?

Why, because the Devil summoned us, he answered.

Wiseman laughed at him, You do not really believe in the Devil?

If not, Simpleton the minister asked, then who summoned us?

Wiseman answered him, It is undoubtedly my friend. He just wants to see me and so he concocted a ruse to summon me.

But then how did he get past all the guards? Simpleton asked.

No doubt he bribed them, and they knowingly lied about it, Wiseman answered.

Thereupon, a man entered and again announced, The Devil has summoned you.

This time Simpleton was not frightened. He had no fear because of the protections he had from the wonder worker. He turned to Wiseman and asked, So, what do you say now?

He answered, I say again that I have a friend who is annoyed with me and has made up this ruse to frighten me.

He then stood up and asked the one who had entered, How would you describe the face of the one who sent for us? What colour was his hair, and so forth?

After being told these details, he declared, You see? That is just what my friend looks like.

Simpleton replied, So will you go then?

Yes, he answered, I will. But would you allow me to bring a few soldiers to serve as bodyguards to protect me from trouble out there?

So Simpleton gave him some guards to accompany him.

Wiseman met his friend, the wise man, and the two went off with the man who had entered before to summon him. Although these wise men could not believe it, the man was dispatched by the Devil himself.

When the bodyguards returned, Simpleton the minister asked where the wise men were. They answered that they had no idea where they had disappeared to. For the messenger of the Devil had snatched the wise men and dragged them off into the muck and mire.

There the Devil sat on his throne in the muck, and this muck was thick and viscous like glue. The wise men could not move in the muck and they shouted, Bandits, why do you torment us? Are we to believe that there is a Devil in the world that torments us for no reason?

The wise men still could not bring themselves to admit the existence of the Devil, so they maintained that it was a gang of bandits that was tormenting them. The two were left stuck in the viscous muck ruminating over their situation, This could only be those scoundrels whom we came to blows with before and now they are tormenting us like this.

So the wise men stayed stuck in the muck for some years, suffering extraordinary torment and torture.

Once, Simpleton the minister was passing by the wonder worker's house and he thought about his old friend Wiseman.

He went into the wonder worker's and bowed to him, as is the custom, and inquired if the wonder worker could possibly find a way to his friend and bring him back. He asked the wonder worker, Do you recall the wise man whom the Devil summoned and then carried off, never to be seen again?

The wonder worker replied, Yes, I recall.

Simpleton the minister asked if he could point the way to the place Wiseman was in order to extricate him.

The wonder worker said, I certainly can show you the place and extricate him. But you and I must go alone.

So the two went together. The wonder worker did what only he knew to do and they arrived. Simpleton saw how the men were stuck in the thick muck and mire. As soon as Wiseman saw Simpleton, he cried out to him, See, my brother, how they beat me and how these bandits torture me so savagely for no reason!

The minister shouted back, You continue to cling to your cleverness and refuse to believe in anything! You think these here are people? But now look: here is the wonder worker whom you once repudiated. Will you at last see that none other than he could point the way here to get you out and lead you to the truth?

Simpleton asked the wonder worker if he could take them out of there and show them that this was indeed the work of the Devil and not of any human being.

So the wonder worker did what he did—and they found themselves suddenly standing on dry land and free of the muck. The demons turned to mere dust.

Then, for the very first time, the wise man recognized the truth and had to concede before everyone that there was, indeed,

a king and that there was, indeed, a genuine wonder worker who
worked genuine wonders.

Look deep
into this tale and you will see wonder upon wonder.
If ever your devotion seems lacking,
it is but a three-sided shoe.
Know this

TENTH TALE

Of a Wealthy Merchant and a Poor Man

A story:

O NCE THERE WAS a merchant who was very wealthy. He traded in a great deal of merchandise, with promissory notes and correspondence all over the world, and was the owner of all manner of good things. Humbler than he lived a poor man who was very poor indeed. He was the exact opposite of the merchant, except that both were childless.

Once, the merchant dreamt that a mob descended upon his home and began to pack up bundle after bundle of his things. He asked them, What are you doing? They replied that they were going to carry it all away to the poor man. This nettled him a great deal and he became angry, but he could not stand up to them because they were so many. But the mob went on packing bundle after bundle of his possessions, merchandise and chattels. They took it all away to the poor man, leaving him only the bare walls. It exasperated him.

Then he woke up and saw it had been a dream. Even though he knew it was only a dream and, praise God, he still had all his possessions, he was nevertheless deeply rattled and he could not get the dream out of his mind.

It had been the wealthy merchant's custom to provide for the poor man and his wife and to give them gifts. Now, after the dream, he provided more for them than before. But whenever the poor man or his wife paid him a visit, he would recall the dream and his face contorted with fear.

The poor man and his wife would often come to his house. One time, the poor man's wife visited to collect something from him. His face contorted and he recoiled in fear. She asked him, Begging your pardon, but tell me, why is it that whenever we come to see you, you cringe so? He told her the story of what he had dreamt and that since then he had been deeply unsettled.

Did this dream take place on this day? she asked, mentioning a date.

He replied, Yes, why?

She said, That same night I, too, had a dream. In it I was a very wealthy woman and people came into my house and started packing up bundle after bundle. I asked them, Where are you going to take all this? They replied, To the poor man—meaning you, sir. But why pay so much attention to a dream? After all, a dream is just a dream.

The merchant was more frightened than ever, and bewildered to boot, now that he had also heard her dream. It seemed to presage his wealth and possessions being brought to the poor man and the poor man's poverty being brought to him. He was terribly frightened.

And it came to pass...

One day the merchant's wife set out on a drive in her carriage. She was accompanied by her lady friends and she also let the poor man's wife tag along. An army general and his regiment happened to be marching by, so the ladies yielded the road to let them pass. The general noticed that it was a group of women travelling. He ordered one of them be snatched away, so the troops went and seized the poor man's wife. They stashed her in the general's coach and rode off. Bringing her back was surely impossible since they had ridden so far away, and even more so because it was a general and his regiment.

The general brought her to his country. She was a God-fearing woman; she did not wish to yield to him and wept greatly. No matter how she was entreated and enticed, she was exceedingly pious.

The merchant's wife and the rest of her entourage returned from their outing and the poor man's wife was not among them. The poor man wept bitterly and tore his hair, lamenting ever for his wife.

One time, the merchant was passing in front of the poor man's house and heard the poor man's bitter, anguished weeping, so he went inside and asked him, Why are you weeping so bitterly?

He replied, What else can I do? What do I have left? Some have wealth, some have children, but I have nothing. Now I have been deprived of my wife as well. So what do I have left?

The merchant was deeply moved and pitied the poor man greatly because he saw his anguish and how very sad he was. The merchant went and did an extraordinary thing; indeed, it was sheer madness. He went and inquired as to what country the general lived in. There he travelled and did a most extraordinary thing: he walked right up to the general's house. The general's guards were stationed in front, yet, in his bewilderment he paid no attention to them. The guards were equally frightened and upset to see someone so bewildered before them. How had he got there?

In all the hubbub he slipped past the guards, entered the general's house, and found the place where the poor man's wife was being kept. He came and woke her and said to her, Come. When she saw him she grew frightened. So he said, Come with me right away. She did so, and the two of them slipped past all the guards until they eluded them.

The merchant then looked around and realized what an extraordinarily brazen thing he had just done. He knew an uproar would instantly ensue at the general's. And so it did. The merchant and the poor man's wife went and hid in a cistern to wait for the commotion to subside. There they stayed for two days. She understood the risk he had taken for her sake and the misery he had suffered over her. So she swore by God that whatever good fortune she might yet achieve, whatever honour and prosperity, none of it would she refuse the merchant. And should he wish to take all of her future prosperity and honour, leaving her as she had been before, she vowed it still should not be refused him. But how could a witness be found there to solemnize her oath? So she took the cistern as a witness. After two more days they left the cistern and continued on their way.

They went on and on, and he realized that in each place they arrived, she was still being sought, too. So he went and hid with her in a mikveh, as they had before in the cistern. She once again recalled the risk he had taken and the misery he had suffered for her sake and, as she had before, swore upon her future good fortune, taking the mikveh as a witness. They remained there for another two days or so and left to continue on their way. Once again he realized that there, too, they were looking for her, and they went and hid again. This happened several more times. Each time they hid in a different place until they had hidden in seven different watery locales, to wit: in a cistern, a mikveh, a marsh, a spring and in streams, rivers and seas. In each place they sought refuge, she remembered the risk he had taken and the misery he had suffered for her sake and she swore never to refuse him her future good fortune. And each time she took that place as a witness. They proceeded in this way, hiding from place to place, until they reached the sea. The merchant was well versed in commerce and knew the maritime trade routes. He was determined to get back to his country, which he did. He returned home with the poor man's wife, delivering her to her husband, and there was much rejoicing.

Since the wealthy merchant had withstood the test of temptation, fearing God and never laying a hand on the poor man's wife, he was remembered by Blessed God and that very year had a son. And for having withstood temptation with the general and with the merchant, the poor man's wife, too, was deemed worthy and bore a daughter. This daughter was a person of extraordinary beauty, indeed, otherworldly beauty—no such beauty existed among mortals. People could hardly wait to see how such an extraordinary marvel would mature. Everyone would say, If only she would mature! Such was the nature of her beauty that no one had ever seen its like before. People came to visit just to catch a glimpse of her and were flabbergasted at her profoundly extraordinary beauty. They would give her presents out of adoration. There was such a flow of gifts that the poor man grew rich.

The merchant's son and the poor man's daughter both regularly studied languages and other subjects in the same class. And the merchant took a notion to arrange a marriage between the two. He thought that perhaps this was the meaning of his dream, where all his things were being carried away to the poor man and all the poor man's things were being carried away to him. Maybe the meaning was that the children were to be betrothed and their households would be merged together.

One time, the poor man's wife came to see the merchant. He told her it was his desire that their children be betrothed and perhaps, thereby, his dream would be fulfilled.

She replied, I, too, had that in mind, but I did not have the impertinence to suggest it. But if you want that, I am certainly willing. I cannot refuse you anything as I have sworn that none of my possessions or prosperity will be refused you.

Among those who used to come to see the poor man's daughter on account of her exceptional beauty were noblemen, whom she pleased greatly. Her beauty was such an extraordinary wonder to them because it was no human beauty. It occurred to these noblemen that they should arrange a marriage for her. One of the nobles had a son, and he desired to arrange a match between her and his own son. But the rest of the noblemen thought a match with such a poor family was beneath their fellow noble-man's dignity. To that end, they lobbied for the poor man's status to be elevated, and they saw to it that he would serve the emperor's court. First he became a lieutenant, and then higher and higher he rose. They saw to his speedy ascent until he became a general. Then, at last, all the noblemen wished to arrange a marriage with him. But there were many noblemen with the same desire since they had all worked hard to elevate him to that end. Moreover, the erstwhile poor man could not arrange such a match because of the merchant, as a match had previously been agreed with him.

The poor man who had become a general went on to greater and greater success. The emperor dispatched him to fight in his wars, and each time he was victorious. So the emperor kept promoting him to ever loftier heights. At last, the emperor died. The whole country then decided the formerly poor man should be appointed emperor. All the noble electors assembled and agreed that he should be the emperor, so he became the emperor. He waged wars and was victorious. He conquered countries and waged further wars, in all of which he was victorious. He kept capturing countries until all other countries peaceably submitted to him, because they saw that his capacity for victory was very great, that all the world's bounty and all the world's good fortune were with him. All their kings gathered together and agreed that he should be emperor of the entire world. And they presented him his mandate inscribed in golden letters.

The emperor no longer wished to arrange a marriage with the merchant, for it was beneath the dignity of an emperor to arrange a match with the family of a merchant. But his wife, the empress, would not forsake the merchant. The emperor saw that he could not arrange a new match for his daughter because of the merchant, especially since his wife was so steadfast in her loyalty to him. So he began to devise plots against the merchant. At first, he thought to impoverish him and devised stratagems to make it seem he was not involved in such plots. And an emperor can surely do such things. The merchant was made to keep suffering losses and haemorrhaging money until he was reduced to poverty and had become an utterly destitute man. The empress, however, remained steadfast in her support for the merchant.

The emperor then realized that as long as the merchant's son lived, he could make no other marriage match for his daughter. So he intervened to put an end to the young man and devised stratagems to do so. He circulated slanders about him and appointed judges to indict him. The judges understood that it was the emperor's will that the young man be done away with, so they issued their sentence that he be put in a sack and cast into the sea.

The empress's heart was most distressed at this, but even an empress can do nothing in defiance of an emperor. So she went to the men who were charged with throwing him into the sea and fell at their feet, pleading with them to let him go for her sake. Why should he be put to death? She implored them to take some other condemned prisoner and throw him into the sea instead and let the young man go. She convinced them, and they swore to her that they would let him go. And that they did. They took another person and threw him into the sea, then they released the young man and told him, Go now, go! And he fled far away. He was, after all, a sensible young man.

Before the young man had escaped his sentence, the empress had called her daughter and told her, My daughter, you must know that the merchant's son is your betrothed.

She went on to tell her the whole story of what had happened to her, saying, The merchant risked himself for my sake. We hid in seven watery places and each time I swore by God that nothing I possessed would be refused him. I took those seven places as witnesses. So you, my most precious, my fortune and happiness, your life is surely indebted to him, and his son is your betrothed. Because of his arrogance, your father wants to murder him. I have intervened to save him and convinced his executioners to let him go. That is why you must know that he is your intended bridegroom and that you must not take any other.

She accepted what her mother had said because she, too, was a God-fearing woman. She replied to her mother that, of course, she would do as her mother had bidden. She went and sent a letter to the merchant's son, who was then in prison, telling him that she considered herself his and that he was her betrothed. She enclosed a rudimentary map and on it she sketched all the locations where her mother and his father had hidden together, with an accurate likeness of each of the seven witnesses. She warned him fervently to protect that scroll with the utmost care. She signed her name below.

Thereupon, the young man, having averted his planned execution with another prisoner taken in his stead, was released and he fled. He kept going until he reached the sea, where he boarded a ship and set sail. A gale rose and drove the ship to a desert shore. Because of the force of the gale the ship was destroyed, but the crew survived and made it to dry land. It was a wasteland, so they went off to find something to eat, each one on his own. As it was a wasteland, ships were not accustomed to stopping there. As a result, they did not expect any ships to come and return them home. So each, taking to his own way, dispersed into the wasteland to find something to eat.

The young man likewise went off into the wasteland. He walked on and on until he was very far from the coast and wished to return but found he could not. The more he wanted to return, the more remote became his possibility of returning. So he kept walking deeper into the wasteland. He fashioned a bow that he used to protect himself from the wild beasts of the wasteland. He walked on and found something to eat. He kept walking and walking until he had left the wasteland and arrived at a place that had been abandoned. There he found water and fruit trees all around. He ate of the fruit and drank of the water. He decided that he would stay there in order to survive, for it was simply too difficult to return to the coast. And who knew whether he might find another settlement were he to leave this one? So he decided to stay there and live out his life. After all, it was good there—he had fruit to eat and water to drink. And periodically he would go out and shoot his bow to catch a hare or a hart for meat. And other times he would go and catch fish because there were very good fish in that water. It pleased him that he would live out his years there.

Now the sentence on the merchant's son had been carried out and he was rid of him, the emperor could finally arrange a match for his daughter. They began proposing matches to her with various kings. He built a seraglio for her, as was their custom, where she dwelt. She brought along ladies, the daughters of noblemen, to be with her there. She would play instruments, as was their custom, and when matches were proposed she would always answer that she did not wish to speak of such things unless the would-be groom came himself. She was very skilled in the art of poetry recitation. She very craftily constructed a balcony to which the would-be groom might climb up to stand before her and recite a poem, a love poem such as a lover recites to his beloved.

Kings came to propose, and they would ascend the balcony, each one reciting his own love poem. To some, she had her ladies deliver her reply, sending a poem and her fond regards. To others who were more pleasing she replied herself, lifting her voice in a poem and answering with words of love. To those who pleased her even more, she appeared in person, showing her face, and answering with an especially affectionate poem. And to each of them she always concluded, But the waters are not gone over you and one night his song shall be with me! No one understood what she meant by this. Moreover, when she showed her face the suitor would swoon on account of her great beauty. Some fainted away and others went mad with lovesickness because of her profoundly extraordinary beauty. Nevertheless, despite all the madness and fainting, kings continued to come to propose to her, and she answered them all in the same way.

The young man had settled in his oasis and made a dwelling to live in. He, too, knew how to play musical instruments and was versed in the art of poetry. He chose wood suitable for instruments and fashioned them from it. From the sinews of beasts he made strings. And he would play music. He would take the letter his betrothed had sent him in prison and he would sing and play and remember everything that had happened to him: from when his father was a wealthy merchant to how he had now come to be there. He took the letter and made a mark on one of the trees. And in that tree he hollowed out a hiding place and hid the letter within. And there he stayed for some time.

Once there arose an immense gale that knocked down all the trees that stood there. He could not identify the tree where he had hidden the letter. When the trees had been standing, he had a mark to recognize, but now that they had fallen, that tree was jumbled together with the numerous other trees. So he could no longer identify his tree. Nor was it possible to split open all the trees to look for the letter because there were so many. So he wept bitterly and grieved much. He understood that if he stayed there he would surely go mad from his anguish. He decided he had to move on, and let whatever might happen happen. He put some meat and fruit in a sack and departed whither he might go, making signs on the place he had left behind.

He travelled on until he came to a settlement and asked, What country is this?

They answered, and next he asked, Have you heard of the emperor?

They replied, Yes.

He asked, Have you heard of his daughter, the great beauty?

They answered, Yes, but no one can win her hand.

Since he could not go to her he came to a decision. He went to the ruler of the kingdom in which he found himself and unburdened his heart, telling him that the emperor's daughter was his betrothed and how she had promised to take no other groom. Because he could not enter the emperor's realm he entrusted the king with all the signs he had, namely the seven watery places, so the king might go there and betroth her, in return for which he would be given money.

The king recognized that he spoke the truth because such a tale was impossible to fabricate. The plan pleased the king, but he decided to have her for himself instead. But keeping the young man around was no good. Should he kill him? No, he did not wish to do such a thing; why should he be killed after the favour he had done him? So the king decided to banish him to a distance of two hundred miles.

The young man was vexed at having been banished for such a favour as he had done for the king. So he went to another king and unburdened himself in the same way, revealing to him the seven signs to which he added one more sign. He enjoined the king, urging him to leave at once with all due haste so he might overtake the other king and arrive there before him. And even if he did not get there first, he had one sign more than the first king. The second king decided as the first king had and likewise banished the young man another two hundred miles away.

Once again, the young man was vexed, so he went to a third king and did as before, giving him further signs, excellent signs indeed.

The first king rose and straight away betook himself to the emperor's daughter's seraglio, where he composed a poem, artfully weaving the seven places into it. But owing to the artistry of the poem, the places were not given in the right order because the prosody demanded otherwise. The king ascended the balcony for declamation and recited his poem. When she heard the seven places she was overcome with astonishment. She was overjoyed: this was certainly her groom! But she was puzzled as to why he had not recited the places in the right order. Nevertheless, she thought, perhaps it was for prosodic effect. She felt in her heart that it was he, so she wrote to him that she would betroth him. There was much rejoicing and excitement because the great beauty had found a match, and preparations were begun for the wedding.

In the meantime, the second king arrived in a hurry and was told that she had already been betrothed. He ignored them and said, Nevertheless… Because he had something to tell her that would surely convince her. The second king came and recited his poem. He put all the places in the right order and to them he added one more sign. She asked the first king how he came to know these things. If he were to tell the truth, it would not benefit him, so he replied that he did not know how. She was overcome with astonishment and stood there bewildered because both kings had recounted all the places. How might a person come to know these signs? Nevertheless, she was overjoyed that

the second king would now be her groom, for she had heard
him telling the signs in the right order and adding a further sign.
Perhaps the first king had only hit upon those places for prosodic
effect. But there she remained, wavering in indecision.

The young man, having been banished by the second king,
and being again very vexed, had gone to the third king and
recounted the whole story to him, telling him further excellent
signs. He had unburdened his heart to the king, revealing he
had a map on which all seven places were sketched. So the third
king should sketch all the places on a piece of paper and bring
it to the emperor's daughter. Then the third king, too, banished
the young man a further two hundred miles, and hurried to her
seraglio. When he was told that there were already two kings
there, he replied, Nevertheless… Because he had something to
tell her that would surely convince her. No one had any idea why
she preferred these to the suitors who had come before.

The third king arrived and recited his poem with the excellent signs, far better than the others'. He showed her the paper
with the sketch of all the places. She was dumbfounded with
fear and surprise but was unable to do anything because she
had thought the first king was her intended and then also the
second king. So she said she would believe no one until her own
scroll was brought to her.

The young man reflected on how far he kept being banished.
So he decided he would simply go there himself—perhaps he
might prevail. So he journeyed until he arrived at the seraglio and
said he had something to tell her that would surely convince her.
He came and recited his poem and included even more excellent

signs. He reminded her that they had studied together in the same class, and revealed yet more signs. He told her everything: how he had sent the three kings and how he had hidden her scroll in a tree and everything that had happened to him.

She turned a blind eye to this. Surely the kings would have their own reasons for why they did not have her scroll, and surely it would be impossible to recognize the merchant's son after such a long time? She would not heed any signs until she was brought the scroll written in her own hand. After all, she had thought the first king was her groom, and then also the second king and the third.

The young man determined that he could not tarry there long lest the emperor catch wind of his presence and kill him, so he decided to return to his place in the wasteland and live out his years there. He travelled on and on to get to the wasteland and eventually arrived. Many years passed, and the young man remained steadfast in his intention to stay there in the wasteland to live out his years. Given his appraisal of man's whole life upon the earth, he arrived at the conclusion that it was fitting to live out his years in that wasteland. So there he stayed, eating fruit and all the rest.

Upon the sea there was a pirate. When this pirate heard tell of an exceptionally beautiful woman in the world, he set his heart on abducting her. Even though he had no physical desire for her, since he had been castrated long ago, he still wished to abduct her in order to sell her to a king. She would fetch a hefty sum of money. The pirate began plotting her abduction. Pirates are impulsive, so he decided to risk it. If he succeeded, he succeeded. And if he did not, so be it. He was impulsive the way pirates are.

He went and bought an extraordinarily large quantity of goods. He crafted golden birds so artfully that people believed they were real, as lifelike as actual birds. Then he made golden ears of corn. And the birds stood on the corn. It was an extraordinary thing for the birds to stand on the corn and the corn not to break, since the birds were quite large. He then cleverly engineered the birds so that they seemed to play, this one trilling, that one chirruping, and that one warbling. All this was achieved by clever tricks—there were men stationed in a room on the ship behind the birds, pulling strings to make it look as if the birds themselves were playing and singing and everything else.

The pirate travelled with all this to the country where the emperor's daughter lived. He arrived at her city and anchored his ship in the port. He pretended to be a great merchant, and people would board the ship to purchase his expensive wares. He stayed there for some time, a full season or more, and people continued to carry off the valuable merchandise they had purchased from him. The emperor's daughter, too, desired to buy goods from him, so she sent for him to bring her some goods. He replied that it was not worth his time to bring goods to a customer's home—even if she were an emperor's daughter. Whoever needed his wares could come to him; no one could compel a merchant in such things. So the emperor's daughter decided to go to him. When she walked in the marketplace it was her habit to veil her face so no one might look at her, as people were liable to swoon because of her beauty. The emperor's daughter went with her face veiled, bringing her ladies with her while a guard trailed behind. She arrived at the merchant-pirate's, purchased some goods, and left. He said to her, When you return, I will show you things more beautiful than these, very fine things indeed. She returned home. Some time later, she came back, bought more goods from him, and once more returned home. The pirate remained there for some time. In the meantime, the emperor's daughter grew accustomed to visiting him and often went to see him.

Once, she came to him, and he went and opened the room where the golden birds stood to show her. She saw what an extraordinary marvel it was. The rest of her entourage also wanted to enter the room, but he said, No, no. I will not show this to anyone except you, for you are the emperor's daughter. I will show it to nobody else.

She alone entered the room. Then he, too, went in and locked the door. He behaved brutishly, taking a sack and forcing her into it. He removed all her clothes, then dressed a member of his crew up in them, veiling the sailor's face and pushing him out on deck, saying, Go!

The sailor did not know what was going on. The moment he appeared with his face veiled, the guard did not realize that it was he, and they all started to leave with him, thinking it was the emperor's daughter. The sailor went with the guard whither they were leading him, and had no idea where in the world he was until he arrived at the emperor's daughter's dressing room. There his face was uncovered and they saw that it was a sailor, which caused a wild commotion. The sailor was dealt a forceful slap in the face and was then shoved aside since he was not responsible, nor did he know anything about the plot.

The pirate took the emperor's daughter and, knowing he would be pursued, left the ship and hid with her in a cistern until the commotion subsided. He ordered the crew of his ship to cut their anchors straight away and flee because they were sure to be pursued immediately. The ship would not be fired upon as long as the emperor's daughter was believed to be aboard.

But they will pursue you, the pirate went on, which is why you have to flee at once. If they should capture you, what do I care?

Such is the manner of pirates. They take risks, and so it was. There was a great commotion, and they were pursued at once, but she was not found aboard.

The pirate hid with her in the cistern. There they lay, and he menaced her into keeping silent so that no one would hear her scream. He said to her, I have risked my life for your sake so that I might capture you, and if I were to lose you, and they take you from me, my life would be worth nothing to me. So if you let out as much as a single cry I will strangle you on the spot, no matter what may happen to me. Out of her fear of him, she remained too frightened to scream.

Some time later, they left the cistern and he led her into the city. They walked on and on and came to another place. The pirate discerned that they were being searched for there as well, so he hid them again, this time in a mikveh. Later on they left there, too, and went somewhere else, where he hid them in another watery place. They kept hiding in this way in different watery places until they had hidden in all the same places the merchant had once hidden with her mother. They did this until they came to the sea. There the pirate searched for anything they could sail in to cross the sea with her, even a little fishing boat. He found such a boat and took the emperor's daughter aboard. He did not desire her, since he was a eunuch, but he wanted to sell her to a king. He was afraid lest she be taken from him. So he went and dressed her in sailor's clothes so she appeared to be a man. The pirate sailed away with him. Suddenly, a gale blew up and bore the boat away to a coast. The vessel was destroyed but they made it to shore, which led to the same wasteland where the young man was living.

When they arrived and the pirate had learnt the lay of the land, the way marauders do, he realized that this place was a wasteland where no ships came. As a result, he had no one to fear and released her bonds. They went off, the marauder this way and the emperor's daughter that way, to find something to eat. She eluded the marauder, and he went on his way until he noticed that she was no longer nearby. So he started yelling for her. She considered his yells but did not reply, thinking, I will end up being sold by him. Why should I answer him? If he reaches me I will tell him I did not hear him, especially as he does not intend to kill me since he wants to sell me.

So she did not answer him and kept walking. The pirate searched for her everywhere. Unable to find her, he kept walking. Presumably, he was devoured by wild beasts.

She continued on and on and found something to eat. She walked until she came to the oasis where the young man was living. Her hair had grown long and shaggy, and, what is more, she was still dressed like a man in sailor's clothes. So they did not recognize one another. As soon as she arrived, he grew merry that another person had joined him.

He asked her, Where did you come from?

She replied, I was accompanying a merchant on the sea. Where did you come from?

He answered likewise, By way of a merchant.

There they both stayed.

After the emperor's daughter had been kidnapped, the empress mourned bitterly and tore her hair over the loss of her daughter. She plagued the emperor with her words, saying, It is because of your arrogance that you dispatched that young man, and now our daughter is lost. She was the whole of our good fortune and our prosperity, and now we have lost her. What do I have left?

She scolded him harshly. He, for his part, was miserable over the loss of his daughter. Add to that the empress sternly rebuking and vexing him, and there were serious quarrels and arguments between them. She said such cruel things to him until she had made him terribly angry and he ordered her to be banished. He appointed judges who ruled she be banished, and so she was.

Some time later, the emperor sent his armies to war, but he was not victorious. So he blamed a general, saying, Because you have done this, we have lost the war. Then he banished the general. Later, he again sent his armies to war, and again he was not victorious and banished another general. In this way he banished a number of generals. The people of his realm saw that he was behaving outlandishly. First he had banished the empress and then the generals. So they discussed whether they ought to do the opposite: send for the empress and banish the emperor. Then the empress would rule the country. And that they did. They exiled the emperor and brought back the empress, and she ruled the country. The empress immediately ordered that the merchant and his wife, whom the emperor had degraded and impoverished, be brought back, and she took them into her palace.

Once he had been banished, the emperor asked the ones who had led him away to let him go, saying, I was your emperor after all. I surely did favours for you. Now, oblige me and let me go, for I will certainly not return to our country. Have no fear; let me go. Let me be off. Allow me my freedom to live out the little time I have left.

They let him go, and he walked on and on.

Many years passed and the emperor had walked on and on until he reached a sea port. The wind also drove his ship to that same desert shore, and he came to the place where the merchant's son and the emperor's daughter, still dressed as a man, were living. None of them recognized each other, because many years had passed and all of them were overgrown with hair.

They asked him, Where did you come from?

He replied, By way of a merchant.

They answered likewise, and the three of them lived there together, eating and drinking and playing musical instruments, since they all knew how to play—he being an emperor and they having learnt together with their tutor.

The young man was the most capable of them for he had been there the longest. He would bring them meat and they would eat. They would burn wood, which in that settlement was more precious than gold. The young man would insist, It is good to live out your years here. Compared to how people live in the so-called civilized world, it is far better here. Here you can live out your lives.

They asked him, What was it like for you before, such that it is better for you here?

He replied, telling them the facts of what had happened to him: from how he was a merchant's son to how he had come to be there. Whatever good things he once had as a merchant's son, he had good things now as well. And he kept insisting to them that it was good to live out their lives there.

The emperor asked the young man, Have you heard of the emperor? He answered that he had. He then asked him about the beautiful daughter and whether he had heard of her? He answered, Yes.

When they spoke of the emperor, whom the young man was unaware he was addressing, he began gnashing his teeth and said angrily, That bandit!

The emperor asked, Why is he a bandit?

The young man replied, It is because of his cruelty and arrogance that I came to be here.

He asked him, How is that?

The young man decided that he had no one to fear here, so he told him the whole story of what had happened to him.

The emperor asked him, If the emperor were here within your reach would you take your revenge on him?

Being a merciful person, the young man replied, No. Instead I would provide for him the way I am providing for you.

Remembering how his beautiful daughter was lost and how he himself had been banished, the emperor began to sigh and groan, and said, What a foul and bitter old age the emperor must have!

The young man replied, It is through his cruelty and arrogance that he brought about his own loss and that of his daughter, and that I ended up here. It is all because of him!

The emperor asked him again, If he were to come within your reach, would you not take your revenge on him?

The young man answered, No. I would provide for him precisely the way I am providing for you.

The emperor then revealed to him that he was that emperor, and explained everything that had happened to him. The young man fell at his feet, then hugged and kissed him. The emperor's daughter was listening to everything the two of them had been saying to one another.

It was the young man's daily habit to go and put a sign on three trees in his search for the scroll. Since there were legions of trees, he would put a sign on the three trees that he searched at a time so that the next day he would not need to look in those trees. He did that every day in case he might eventually find the scroll. Whenever he returned, his eyes were full of tears, for he would weep at having searched and having been unable to find it.

The other two asked him, What are you looking for among the trees that you always return with tears in your eyes?

He told them the whole story, about how the emperor's daughter had sent him a letter, he had hidden it in one of the trees, and a gale had knocked down all of the trees. Now he was searching for it.

They said to him, Tomorrow, when you go looking, we shall come with you. Perhaps we might find the scroll.

So it was. They went out with him, and the emperor's daughter found the scroll in one of the trees. She opened it up and saw that it was in her own hand. She reflected, if she revealed right away that she was the emperor's daughter, then when she took off those sailor's clothes and returned to her former beauteous state, and was once more a beautiful woman as before, he might collapse from the shock and die. But she wanted their wedding to be in accordance with the law and could not marry him in the wasteland, as she needed the wedding to be bona fide. So she went and returned the scroll to him, telling him only that she had found it. He fell instantly in a faint. They revived him, and there was much rejoicing among them.

Later, the young man said, What good does this scroll do me? How will I be able to find her? Having been abducted and sold, as the emperor related, she will surely now be with some king. So what good is this to me? I am going to live out my years here.

So he went and returned the scroll to her and said, Here, you take this scroll and see if you may marry her.

As she set about preparing to leave she asked him to go with her, saying, As I shall surely marry her, all will be well with me, so I shall give you a portion of my property.

The young man saw that this sailor was a wise man and that he would surely find and marry her. So he agreed to accompany him. The emperor, however, chose to remain by himself because he was afraid to return to his country. The sailor, that is the emperor's daughter, also asked him to accompany them as he would surely marry the beautiful woman, saying, You have nothing to fear, since your luck will return when she is found and you will be called upon to return.

All three of them went together until they hired a ship and travelled to the country where the empress dwelt. Arriving in the city where she resided, they moored the ship. The empress's daughter reflected, if she revealed right away to her mother that she had come, her mother might die from the shock of it. So instead she sent word to her mother that there was a person who had news of her daughter. Then she herself went to the empress and told her what had happened to her daughter, recounting the whole story. At the end she said, And she is here, too!

Then she revealed the truth: I am she!

She informed her that her intended groom, the merchant's son, was also there. But she told her mother that she did not want anything but that her father, the emperor, be allowed to return to his place. Her mother did not want that, for she was still very angry at him because all of this had been his fault. But she had to oblige her daughter. They wished to return. The emperor was sought in the place he was meant to be banished, but he could not be found there. The princess revealed that the emperor, too, was with her and her intended.

The wedding took place, and the rejoicing was fulsome. The merchant's son and the beautiful woman took their place on the throne of the empire, and they reigned over the world.

Amen and Amen

ELEVENTH TALE

Of a Prince and a Handmaid's Son

A story:

ONCE THERE WAS a king in whose household was a hand-maid who served the queen. Ordinarily, no vulgar scullery maid would be permitted into the king's inner sanctum; however, this handmaid was a servant of no common rank.

The time came when the queen was to have a child. The handmaid, too, was going to give birth. Just to see what would come of it, the midwife went and switched their babies. She took the king's child and laid it down beside the handmaid, and she took the handmaid's child and laid it beside the queen.

The children grew. The prince (that is, the child they thought a prince) was raised to higher and higher positions until he was very great and a man of immense talent. The handmaid's son (that is, the child who was being brought up by the handmaid) grew up with her. The two children studied together in the same class. It was in the nature of the true prince (who was called the handmaid's son) to be drawn to the trappings of royalty, although he was raised in a humble servant's home. It was exactly the opposite for the handmaid's son (who was called the prince), whose nature was to be drawn to less than regal trappings despite being brought up in the king's home. Yet, he had to conform to a more royal comportment because that was how he had been shown to behave.

Since, as our sages of old have taught, the female mind is flighty and women are incapable of restraint, the midwife went and revealed to someone the secret of how she had switched the children. Now, everyone has a friend, and that friend has a friend. One person divulged the secret to another in this way until it had become public knowledge, as is the way of the world. People certainly could not engage in wanton gossip about how the prince had been switched, lest the king learn of it, so they did so on the sly. What would the king do if he found out? He could not remedy the situation. He might well not believe it. What if it were a lie? How could they be switched back? Clearly the king must never find out. But people kept gossiping about it on the sly.

And it came to pass...

A person went and revealed to the ostensible prince that people were saying he had been switched at birth.

But you cannot dwell on this, the person went on, for it is beneath you. And what good would dwelling on it serve? I told you this so that you should know in case one day there might be a rebellion against the kingdom, and the rebellion were to reinforce itself by saying they were taking the prince, that is, the one they declared to be the true prince, as their king. So you must see to devising a way of dealing with this young man.

So the ostensible prince started playing tricks on the young man's father, who was in fact his own father, in a constant effort to do him harm. He inflicted one mischief after another on him to drive him and his son away. As long as the king was still alive, the ostensible prince's power was limited. Yet, nevertheless, he kept playing his malicious tricks.

The king grew old and died, and the apparent heir apparent acceded to the throne. He went on doing ill to the young man's father, one malicious thing after another, but in such a way that people were unaware that he was the cause, for such behaviour was not seemly for respectable people.

The young man's father understood that the new king was wronging him because of what people were saying about the children having been switched. So he spoke to his son, telling him the whole story. He said to him, I feel great pity for you in either case. If you are my child, I of course feel great pity for you. But if it turns out that you are not my child and are in fact the prince, then I would feel even greater pity for you as the king wants to extirpate you utterly, God forbid. So you must flee.

The young man was greatly troubled by this.

In the meantime, however, the king kept inflicting his torments, one after the other. So the young man decided he had to flee. His father gave him a sum of money and off he went. It nettled him to be driven from his country for no good reason. He considered, Why do I deserve to be driven away? If I am indeed the rightful prince, I certainly do not deserve to be driven away. And even if I am not the prince, I still do not deserve to be made a fugitive for no good reason. What sin am I guilty of?

He became terribly embittered, on account of which he took to drinking and frequenting brothels. He wanted to spend his life in this way, getting drunk and indulging his lust because he had been driven away for no good reason.

The ostensible king took hold of the throne with rigour. When he heard that people were muttering and gossiping about the switch he punished them with torture, thus taking his revenge on them. He ruled by might and majesty.

And it came to pass...

The king was off with his lords on a hunting party when they came to a lovely spot with a brook running past it. They stopped there to rest and stroll about. The king lay down to nap, when he began contemplating what he had done, driving the young man away for no good reason. In either case: if the young man was indeed the prince, was it not enough that he was switched? Why should he also have been driven away for no good reason? And if he was not the prince, he still did not deserve to be driven away. After all, how had he sinned? Thus the ostensible king pondered the matter and regretted the sin and great injustice he had done, but he was unable to find a solution he could pursue. Such a shameful thing could not be discussed with others, nor could he seek anyone's advice about it. The king was preoccupied with these anxieties and ordered his lords to return home. As the king was so perturbed, it seemed an inopportune time for a carefree stroll, so they all turned back. Once home, the king had various affairs and official business to attend to. Being so engaged in these duties, this other matter slipped his mind.

Meanwhile, the fugitive true prince did what he did and dissipated all his money. One time, he went out for a walk by himself and lay down. Everything that had happened to him came to his mind, and he began to reflect, What has God done to me? If I am indeed the prince, I certainly do not deserve this. And if I am not the prince, then I still do not deserve to be a fugitive and an exile.

He then considered once more, However, if it is in fact the case that Blessed God can do such a thing and swap out a prince and make such things come to pass, ought I still to behave this way? Is what I have done right? Is it proper to conduct myself as I have?

He began to feel immense anxiety and regret over the sinful deeds he had committed. He returned home but again took to drinking. Yet because he had started feeling remorse he often became confused, with thoughts of regret and repentance constantly swirling in his mind.

Once he lay down and dreamt that there was a fair in a certain place on a certain date to which he had to go. The dream instructed him to take the very first opportunity for profit he might chance upon, even if it did not comport with his dignity. Then he woke up, but the dream stuck in his mind. Periodically there were things that slipped his mind, but this dream was firmly lodged there. Even so, it was difficult to achieve, and he again took to drinking. He dreamt the dream several more times, and the dream continued to perplex him.

Once, he was told in his dream, If you seek mercy, do as this dream bids you.

So he had to fulfil it. He gave away whatever money he had left and paid what he owed at the inn where he had been staying.

He left his nice clothes at his lodgings. He rose early, put on simple merchant's attire, and set off for the fair. He met a merchant who asked him, Would you like to earn some money?

He replied, Yes.

The merchant said, I need to drive some cattle. Will you hire yourself out to me?

Because of his dream's injunction to take the first opportunity for profit he might chance upon, he did not think twice. He answered instantly, Yes.

The merchant hired him on the spot and right away started ordering him around, the way a lord does his servants. The young man now began to reconsider what he was doing there, because he certainly did not deserve such servitude, for he was a person of refinement. Now he was going to have to drive cattle and walk alongside them to do so. But he could not back out. The merchant ordered him around like a lord, whereupon the young man asked him, Am I to walk on my own with the cattle?

The merchant replied, No, I have other herdsmen who drive the cattle. You will walk along with them.

The merchant handed several head of cattle over to him to drive, and he drove them out of the city, whereupon he met the rest of the herdsmen driving their cattle. They all walked on together. The young man drove his cattle by foot as the merchant rode alongside them on horseback. The merchant pressed them all cruelly, and he was especially cruel to the young man. He grew ever more frightened of the merchant because he could clearly see the degree of cruelty and abuse the merchant heaped on him. Being a person of refinement, he was afraid lest the merchant deal him a blow with his staff powerful enough to kill him. So he walked on among the cattle with the merchant alongside until they came to a place to rest. A sack was passed around and bread distributed. The young man, too, was given some, and he ate.

Afterwards, they were travelling through a dense forest and two cows went astray. The merchant yelled at him, so he and some of the herdsmen went to look for the cattle. The cows had fled quite a distance, so he pursued them. Since the forest was so dense, none of them could see the others, each person hidden from the others' sight. The young man kept on in pursuit of his two missing cows. They continued to flee and he continued to go after them until he arrived in an especially dense part of the forest.

He reflected, No matter what, I am going to die. If I return without the cows, the merchant will kill me. And if I stay here, the beasts of the forest will get me.

So he considered, How can I go back to face the merchant without his cows?

Because of his great fear of the merchant, he continued to pursue the cows, who continued to flee.

Meanwhile, night had fallen. Such a thing had never happened to him before, having to spend the night in such a dense forest. He heard the roaring of the forest beasts, as was their wont. He decided to climb up a tree and spend the night there. From the tree he listened to the sound of the forest beasts, roaring as they do.

In the morning, he looked and saw the cows standing nearby. So he climbed down out of the tree and went to seize them. But on they fled, with him in pursuit. The cows found a grassy patch and stopped to graze. The young man tried to take hold of them, but on they fled. And so it went, over and over again, the young man pursuing and the cows fleeing, until he reached the dense heart of the forest where the beasts had no fear of humans as they were very far from any settlement.

Night fell once more. He heard the sound of the beasts roaring, and he was terrified. He then caught sight of an especially large tree. So he clambered up it. As soon as he had climbed the tree he saw a man lying there. This frightened him, but he also took comfort in it because he had found another person. They began asking questions of one another.

Who are you?

Just a man. Who are you?

Just a man, as well.

Where have you come from?

The young man did not want to explain all that had happened to him, so instead he replied, Two of the cows I was herding strayed into the forest. That's how I came to be here.

He then asked the man he had found in the tree, Where have you come from?

The man answered, I came here on account of my horse. I was riding and stopped to rest. My horse strayed into the forest, so I went after it. But it kept running away until I arrived here.

They took the opportunity to stick together and agreed that even if they were to come to a settlement, they would stay together. The two of them spent the night there in the tree, listening to the sounds of the beasts as they roared and howled.

At dawn, the young man heard the sound of immense laughter over the forest. The laughter was so loud it made the tree shake.

He was terrified. The other man said, That no longer frightens me. I have spent several nights here, and every morning as dawn approaches that laughter is heard, making all the trees tremble and shake.

The young man, still terrified, said to the other man, Apparently this is a demons' place, because in a place where people live you never hear laughter like that. Where in the world has anyone ever heard such laughter?

Dawn came swiftly. The two of them looked and saw the cows and the horse standing there. So they climbed down from the tree and started pursuing their animals, the young man after his cows and the other man after his horse. But the cows fled and the young man pursued them, and the horse fled and the other man pursued it, until they were completely separated and had no idea where the other one was. The young man came upon a sack of bread, which is very important in a wilderness. So he took the sack up onto his shoulder and continued after his cows.

He then encountered a man. At first he was frightened, but then he took some comfort in it because he had found yet another person. The man asked him, How have you come to be here?

He countered, How have you come to be here?

The man replied in surprise, I, my parents, and my parents' parents were raised here. But you, how have you come to be here? No people from town ever come here.

The young man was terrified because he realized that this was no ordinary man. But still, the man from the forest was doing him no harm and so he befriended him.

The man from the forest asked, What are you doing here?

He replied that he was pursuing his errant cattle.

The man from the forest said, Stop pursuing your sins. For it is not your cows but your sins that drive you on. Enough already! You have already done your penance. Now stop pursuing them. Come with me and you will achieve your purpose.

The young man went with him, but he was afraid to speak with him or ask him anything, because a man like that might open his mouth and devour him. So he simply followed.

Later, the young man came across his friend, who was still pursuing his horse. As soon as he saw him he sought to signal to him that the other man was no ordinary man and because of that he should have no dealings with him. He walked up to him and whispered as much in his ear. His friend, meanwhile, had spied the sack of bread on the young man's shoulder and began to beg, Brother! It is many days since I have eaten. Give me some bread.

The young man replied, Here in the wilderness there is nothing I can do for you. I need the bread for myself. I must protect my own life before the life of another.

Despite understanding the young man's explanation, his friend started begging and pleading, I will give you anything at all!

The young man answered, What can you give me for bread in the wilderness?

His friend said, I offer myself to you. I will sell myself to you as a slave for that bread.

The young man reflected that acquiring a person was worth the gift of bread. So the young man purchased him as an eternal slave and made him swear oaths that in exchange for bread he would be his eternal slave, even if they should happen to come to some human settlement. They would both eat bread from the sack until it ran out.

The two of them went on together, the slave after his owner, and followed the man from the forest. Things were somewhat easier for the young man now that he had a slave. If he needed to lift something or do something, he ordered his slave to lift it or to do it. They followed the man from the forest until they reached a place swarming with snakes and scorpions. The young man was very frightened and asked the man from the forest, How will we get past here?

How else? To do so we must head towards my house, the man replied, pointing to a house floating in the air.

They kept following him, and he led them across unharmed and brought them up into his house. He gave them food and drink, and then departed.

The young man ordered his slave around, telling him to do what he needed done. His slave was terribly resentful at having sold himself into slavery on account of that single hour he needed bread. Now he had something to eat, but for the sake of that one hour of need he was to be an eternal slave. He let out a deep sigh. How has it come to this, that I should be a slave?

The young man, his master, asked him, What was your former glory that you can sigh so about how it has come to this?

In reply he told him the story, about how he was a king and how it was rumoured that he had been switched at birth; about how he had driven his erstwhile rival away; about how he was periodically overcome by the idea that he had not behaved justly and felt remorse. His mind was plagued with perpetual regret for his evil deed and for the great injustice he had done.

Once he dreamt that his redress was to abdicate his throne and go wherever his eyes directed him. And so doing, he would expiate his sin. He did not want to do that, initially. But his dreams that he should do so kept confounding him until the idea stuck and, at last, he abdicated the throne. He went his way until he arrived in that place. Now here he was—a slave.

The young man listened to all of this and held his tongue, thinking, I need to consider what to do with you.

That night, the man from the forest returned and gave them food and drink. There they spent the night. At dawn, they heard the immense laughter that made all the trees convulse with trembling. The slave prevailed upon his master to ask the man from the forest what it was. He asked him, What is that immense laughter so close to dawn?

He replied, It is the day laughing at the night. For the night riddles the day, What follows me close like a faithful hound, but is nowhere seen when I turn back around? The day bursts into laughter, and then it is dawn. That is the laughter you hear at daybreak.

The young man was astonished at such an extraordinary thing: the day laughing at the night. He was unable to ask anything else, since the man from the forest had so answered.

In the morning, the man from the forest went off again, leaving them food and drink. At night, he returned. They ate and drank and spent another night. That night, they heard the sound of the beasts roaring and howling with extraordinary noises. The lion roared; the leopard growled, with its own unique sound; the birds whistled and trilled; and each of the remaining beasts bellowed in its own way. At first, they were so frightened they did not listen closely to the sounds. But then they inclined their ears to listen more attentively and they heard it was a melody the beasts were singing, a delightful melody. This was an extraordinary surprise. The more they listened, the greater the extraordinary pleasure it was to hear. All the pleasures of the world amounted to nothing compared to the great pleasure one experienced hearing that wondrous melody. The two discussed it and decided they wished to stay there because they had food and drink and because they took such pleasure in that marvel of a melody such that all the other pleasures of the world were as nothing compared to it.

The slave prevailed upon his master to ask the man from the forest what the wondrous melody was. He asked him, and the man from the forest answered, When the sun, taking its leave, passes its mantle to the moon, all the forest beasts cry out to extoll the great favours the moon does on their behalf. For the dominion of beasts is at night. From time to time they need to enter a human settlement, and, as their dominion is only at night, they cannot do so by day. The moon does them a favour by illuminating the night. For that reason all the beasts come together to make a new melody in honour of the moon. That is the melody you hear.

They listened more closely to attend to the melody. When they listened to this delightful, sweet melody, the man from the forest said to them, If you are so astonished at the beasts' song, you should see this. I have an instrument, a singing box, that

I received from my parents and that they inherited from their parents. The singing box is made from various things and reeds in a variety of colours. When one places it on any animal or bird it can immediately start playing its song.

Then the laughter returned as dawn broke. The man from the forest headed out once again. The young man went looking for the instrument. He searched the whole house but could not find it. He was too fearful to go on looking.

After some time, the two of them—master and slave, the true prince and the supposed king—longed to return to a human settlement, but they were apprehensive about asking the man from the forest to take them. When the man from the forest returned, though, he gladly offered to take them to a settlement, which he did. He had brought along the singing box and gave it to the young man, the true prince, and told him, I grant you this as a gift. And you shall know, he concluded, gesturing to the young man's slave, what to do with this one.

They asked him, Where shall we go?

He replied that they should make inquiries about a country called the Foolish Land with the Wise Regime.

They asked him, What direction should we start making our inquiries about that country?

The man from the forest pointed out the direction and said to the true prince, Go to that country and there you shall achieve your glory.

The two headed off. As they walked they were overcome with a desire to find some beast or animal on which to test whether the singing box would play, but they did not see any animals.

Eventually they came to a settlement and found a cow. They placed the box on the cow, and it began singing the melody.

They went on, walking and walking, until they arrived at that country. But it was surrounded by a wall so that the country could only be entered via a gateway, which one would have to walk several miles to reach. So they walked the several miles and reached the gate. When they approached they were not allowed to pass because the country's king had died, and the prince remained. The king had left a will stating that, whereas up until then the country had been called the Foolish Land with the Wise Regime, henceforth it would be called the opposite, the Wise Land with the Foolish Regime. Whosoever should undertake to reinstate calling it by the previous name would become king. For that reason, entrance into the country was restricted to only the one who vowed to reinstate the country's previous name. They asked the young man, Can you do so?

Obviously he could not do so, so they refused to let him pass. His slave told him they ought to return home. But he was reluctant since the man from the forest had told him he should go to that country and there he would achieve his glory.

Meanwhile, another man arrived, riding a horse. He wished to enter, but, unwilling to undertake that task, he too was not allowed to pass. Having noticed the man's horse standing there, the young man took the singing box and went and placed it on the horse, whereupon it started playing the delightful melody. The man implored him to sell him the box, to which he replied, What could you give me for such a wondrous instrument?

The man asked, What can you do with it? You will just use it for cheap entertainment, perhaps to earn a few gulden. But I know something even more marvellous than your singing box. It is a gift I inherited from my parents' parents: the gift of knowing how to deduce one thing from another. Using this, you can deduce the true meaning hidden behind what anyone says. I have never revealed this to another living soul, but I will teach it to you in exchange for the singing box.

The young man thought, It truly is a wonder to be someone who possesses the power of deduction.

So he gave him the instrument. The man went and taught him how to deduce one thing from another. The true prince lingered by the gate of the country, realizing that now that he had the full power of deduction, it was quite plausible for him to undertake reinstating the country's previous name. So he decided once more to seek entry and then undertake reinstating the country's previous name. What did he have to lose? The men let him in.

The state ministers were informed about the young man. He was brought before the ministers who said, You should know we are no fools, God forbid. But the former king was an extraordinarily sagacious man, and compared to him we were all as fools. That is why the country was once called the Foolish Land with the Wise Regime. Then our king died, and the prince remained. The prince is also wise, but compared to us he is no sage. That is why the country is now called the opposite, the Wise Land with the Foolish Regime. According to the king's will, should such a wise man be found who is similarly extraordinarily sagacious, and compared to whom all are as fools, he would become king and do everything as foretold. You must know what it is you are undertaking.

The ministers of state continued, This is the test of your sagacity. There is a garden here left over from the days of our former king. The garden is an extraordinary marvel. Within it abound metalware vessels, of silver and gold. But no one can enter the garden, for whenever a person tries to enter he is instantly chased. But the person cannot catch sight of his invisible pursuer. He is chased until he flees the garden, shrieking in fear. Thus we shall see if you are a sage by your ability to enter the garden.

He asked, Is he who attempts to enter the garden beaten?

They replied, Mainly he knows he is chased by this unknown pursuer, and he is forced to flee in a panic. At least, so we have been told by those who have attempted to enter before.

The young man rose and walked over to the garden. He saw there was a wall around it and the gate stood open. There were no guards, because such a garden certainly needed none. He approached further and peeked in. He noticed a man standing nearby, rather, it was the statue of a man. He took a closer look and saw there was a tablet above the man on which was inscribed that the man depicted had been king several hundred years earlier. In the days of that king there had been peace. Before and after him there had been war, but during his reign there was peace.

Since he was someone who could deduce one thing from another, the young man understood that it all hinged on that man. When you entered the garden and started to be chased, you did not have to flee. Rather, you could stand next to the statue under his protection. Moreover, were you to take the royal statue and station him in the very midst of the garden, then everyone could enter the garden in peace. So he went and entered the garden. The moment he started to be chased, he went and stood next to the man's statue that stood at the opening of the garden. In this way he made it out in peace and unharmed.

While others who attempted to enter the garden may have been chased off in a panic or, perhaps, beaten, the young man had come out in peace and tranquillity because he had stood near the statue. The ministers of state witnessed his peaceful entry and departure in astonishment. The young man then ordered the statue be taken and placed in the centre of the garden, which it was. The ministers thus entered the garden, walking through it and coming out in peace.

The ministers said to him, Still, even though we have seen you do this, you are not entitled to be given the kingdom on the basis of a single feat. We will test you with one more. Here is the former king's throne. It is very tall. Next to it are all kinds of beasts and birds carved from wood. In front of the throne stands a divan, next to which there is a table, and on the table is a candelabrum. Pathways extend from the chair, and these paths are paved and radiate out in all directions. No one can tell where each path from the throne leads. Where one of the ways extends off into the distance, there a golden lion stands. When someone approaches it, the lion opens its maw as if to devour him. Past the lion, the path extends further. And so, too, for the rest of the roads that radiate from the throne. There is a second road, and where that road extends from the throne stands another beast, this time an iron leopard. It, too, cannot be approached lest it devour you. Past the leopard, the path extends further. And so for the rest of the roads. All these paths extend through the whole country. No one can see where the paths from the throne lead. Therefore, your test will be to determine the true destination of the paths and the true purpose of everything else in the royal chamber.

The young man was shown the throne, and he saw how tall it was and everything else there. He walked over to it to inspect it further. He realized that the throne had been made of the same wood as the singing box the man from the forest had gifted him. He took a closer look and saw its carved top was missing a little rosette. If the throne just had that little rose, he surmised, it might possess the power of the singing box that played the beasts' melody. He kept searching and saw the rosette lying below it. One needed but to take it from under the throne and insert it back on top and it would have the power of the singing box. The former king had arranged each thing with great cunning, everything cleverly concealed so that no one would understand what it meant until such an extraordinarily sagacious man might come who could figure out how to adjust all the things back to their proper arrangement.

With regard to the divan, he understood it needed to be pushed back a little from where it now stood. The table, too, needed to be moved somewhat away from its current spot. As did the candelabrum. The birds and the beasts also needed to be moved just a bit. The bird from one spot needed to go in another. Everything was in need of a little adjusting. So, too, the golden lion that stood where one path extended needed to be moved. And everything needed to be rearranged. The young man ordered all the things be moved to where they needed to go, beginning with the little rosette that needed to be taken from beneath the throne and inserted above.

As soon as all this had been done, the delightful melody, which was such an extraordinary marvel, began to ring out. Each piece was now in its proper place, and so the true prince was handed the throne.

He said to the handmaid's son, Now I understand: I really am the true prince and you are, indeed, the handmaid's son.

TWELFTH TALE

Of a Master of Prayer

A story:

ONCE THERE WAS a Master of Prayer, a man whose calling was to lead all in worship. He was wholly devoted to
his task of conducting prayers and hymns and songs of praise
to Blessed God. The Master lived out in the countryside and it
was his custom to come into town, where he might meet with a
particular person or visit with the humble townsfolk, the poor
and the like.

Once there, he would get to chatting with folks about the
point of life and how there was truly no other purpose in the
entire world but to live one's life in devotion to the Almighty.
One ought to spend the length of one's years engaged in worship of Blessed God through prayer and singing hymns and
songs of praise. He would often strike up a conversation about
this, and the minds of those he spoke with would be awakened
as his words pierced their hearts until they happily consented
to join him. As soon as they did, he would lead them off to
his spot in the countryside. He had chosen to live far from
bustling towns and cities, in a place where there was a stream
and orchards of fruit trees and where it did not matter how

one dressed—however one wished to go about was perfectly acceptable.

Such was his practice: he would go into town and talk with the folks there and convince them to follow his path of devotion to God and commit themselves wholly to His worship. He would take those who heeded him and lead them out to his place in the countryside. There, they would pray and sing hymns and songs of divine praise and they would engage in fasting and beating their breasts in confession and in self-denial and repentance. The Master doled out his own compositions of hymns and paeans and penitential prayers, and the people would devote themselves to such prayers continuously. Before long, some among the people that he had brought with him were able to bring yet others into the fold and to Blessed God. The Master would occasionally grant them permission to go into town to awaken the minds of others to the Almighty so that they might serve Him.

So the Master went about in this way, winning people over to his mission and bringing them from towns into the countryside. In due course, he gained a reputation far and wide and began to become quite famous. Suddenly, people were reported missing in the more populated places and no one knew what had become of them. Someone's son or son-in-law would vanish and their whereabouts would be unknown until it was discovered that they were with the Master who went around inducing others to serve Blessed God. But there was no catching him to stop him. For the Master conducted himself cleverly, changing his guise every time. On one occasion he might appear as a pauper and on another as a merchant—always a different disguise.

In addition, if ever he entered into a discussion and realized that he was not winning his listeners over, he would shift topics so that they would never guess his true aim, namely, bringing them to serve Blessed God. They would be hard-pressed even to guess at where the conversation was leading, even though his true intention all along was to bring the people he conversed with to serve the Almighty. This was his singular mission. But if he realized that he might not be convincing them, he would bewilder them with baffling words to obscure his meaning. So it was that the Master could never be caught as he went on this way until he was famous far and wide, and capturing him seemed impossible.

The Master and his people lived out in the countryside, where they were constantly engaged in prayer and songs of worship and praise to the Blessed Lord, and in fasts, self-denial and repentance. The Master also saw to it that he provided all that his followers needed. If he felt that one of his devotees, based on this individual's state of mind, might be better suited to serve God apparelled in gold embroidery, he made sure such was provided. On the other hand, if he had brought a rich man from town into the fold and he felt that this rich man would be better clad in tatters, he knew just what to do. Thus he accommodated the needs of all. To those that he brought to serve Blessed God, fasting and the most stringent forms of self-denial were dearer than any worldly pleasure; indeed, they relished their fasting and self-denial more than any other earthly delight.

And it came to pass...

There was a nation overflowing with wealth. Everyone there was quite rich, but the nation was run in a most outrageous manner. Everything was handled on the basis of wealth. The rank and honours due to anyone were all reckoned according to wealth alone. It was established that so many thousands or tens of thousands of pieces of gold conveyed some particular rank and honour. And if one had even more thousands or tens of thousands, this meant an even higher rank and honour still—all according to the sum of money one had. As for the one who had so many more thousands, tens of thousands, and hundreds of thousands, he was determined to be a king.

What is more, the amount of money one had was signalled by a particular banner. Whosoever, according to his affluence, had a particular rank or honour was given a banner that indicated the rank he held.

It was established that a person's rank, as determined by their overall worth, might cause them to be deemed a common man, but one who had less was not considered a man at all, but rather was ranked a beast or a bird in human form. Thus, beasts and birds walked among the people there. If there was a man who had only a little bit of money, he might be reckoned a lion or a sphinx. If there was a man with less money still, his rank would be a bird. And there were many other beasts and birds, as well, for those who had less money were not considered human. The principal thing, after all, was money, and every rank and every honour was determined by it.

Furthermore, the people of this Nation of Wealth allocated among themselves the ranks of heavenly bodies and constellations.

Whosoever was accounted to have a particular sum of money could be a star, insofar as having so much one had the power of a star, whose dust is the source of the gold that can be extracted from the earth. If a person had such a sum, then he was considered to possess the power of a gold dust-producing star and was, therefore, considered a star himself. So believed the people of the country in their delusion about money.

The people there had similar ideas about constellations. If one had a great sum, he was considered to be a constellatory array of stars. They also designated themselves as angels according to their level of wealth. And eventually they got to calling themselves gods as well. If one had so many thousands and hundreds of thousands, he was determined a god. Since God had granted him so much money, he was considered a god himself.

As the existence of this nation became known in the world and the Master heard about it, he heaved a deep sigh, saying, Who knows how much further these people might stray, believing as they do?

Among his devotees were some who, without even asking the Master's opinion, betook themselves to the Nation of Wealth to set those people on the right path. They had great pity for the nation whose inhabitants were so deluded in their lust for money, especially as the Master had said that they might go even further astray. So it was that the devotees of the Master headed to the nation in order to set them right and lead them away from their folly.

They entered the Nation of Wealth and, sure enough, straight away came across a humble man—considered a beast by the locals—and got to talking with him, saying, Truly, money is not the point of living, but rather the purpose of our lives is to serve God.

But the man would not even listen to them, so deeply rooted was the belief that money was the most important thing in the world. The same thing happened when they went to speak with another countryman. He, too, would not heed them. They wished to continue the conversation, but he told them, Frankly, I have no time to speak with you.

Why not? they asked.

He answered, Because we all have to leave this land to go to another. As money is the sole purpose of life, it has been decided that we ought to move to a place where money is manufactured, where gold and silver can be extracted from the earth to make more money. All of us are set to head out right away.

Moreover, the people of the nation had come to think that the foul air of the earth was not fit for them. Nor were they to associate with people from other countries, lest they be polluted by them, believing as they did that everyone else in the world was impure and could defile them. So they decided that they would look to lofty mountains where they would be higher than the rest of the world and above its foul air.

They had sent people out in search of such heights. When they had at last discovered exceptionally high mountains, the entire country went to live atop them. They settled there in clusters, forming cities on various mountain peaks. They built great fortifications around each peak and a deep ditch around the ramparts. Now it would surely be unthinkable for anyone to discover them, especially since there was but one hidden path that led to their heights, assuring that no outsider could find their way to them. Just so, they fortified all the other peaks and stationed guards at a distance from the mountain so that no one could reach them. They settled atop the peaks and continued their ways as before, with their many gods all determined according to their wealth.

However, since money was the principal thing for them, they lived in perpetual fear of murder and plunder. Why would a person not become a killer or a bandit if he could become a god with the money he stole? Yet, they held, whosoever had enough money to be a god possessed divine protection against murder and plunder. To that end, they initiated rituals and sacrifices in which they made offerings and prayers to the gods for even more money. They would also offer human sacrifices, rendering their fellow countrymen up to the gods so the offerands might be subsumed and become rich in their next incarnation. Indeed, the utmost essence of their faith was money, and they practised these rituals and sacrifices and made burnt offerings to serve their gods—that is, to serve those among them who had great wealth. And yet, the country was utterly full of murder and plunder, as those who did not practise such rituals became killers and bandits in order to acquire more wealth. Money was, after all, the most important thing. Money could buy everything—food and clothes—thus, it was the sine qua non of man's existence. Money was the central tenet of their faith and, just so, constituted their entire foolish, deluded worldview.

They took the greatest care never to lose any money, since it was the essence of their faith and their supreme ruler. Rather, they saw to it that additional wealth would be brought into their country from elsewhere. To that end, some set off to become merchants and conducted business abroad to earn money in order to infuse their nation with even more wealth.

Giving charity was not allowed among them. Who, after all, would dare to give away wealth that was divinely bestowed? Since the most important thing for them was to have money, how could it simply be given away? For this reason, charity was strictly forbidden.

Official assessors were appointed who saw to it that everyone truly had as much money as claimed. Each person was forever obligated to prove his wealth in order to maintain the rank and honours his wealth afforded. That is, all the wealthiest—those who were considered to be gods and stars and angels and the like—were frequently audited to verify whether they had the requisite amount of money and that they were not erroneously considered a god.

Such officials were appointed to look after this regularly and, on occasion, a beast might have to be made a man or a man a beast. For if a rich countryman had lost his money, he was no longer reckoned a man, but rather a beast. And conversely with the beast whose wealth increased—he would then be considered a man. So it was with all the other ranks that were determined according to the sum of money possessed. From time to time it also happened that one ceased to be a god because of the loss of his fortune. For those who remained gods, however, portraits and icons were made of them, which the people would embrace and kiss. Indeed, money was the central object of their veneration and basis of their faith.

The group of the Master's devotees who visited the nation returned to their place in the countryside. They told the Master all about the nation's follies: how the people there were so bamboozled and had gone so far astray in their love of money; how they were to leave their own land for another where they could extract materials to make more money; and how they appointed themselves stars and constellations. The Master responded that he was afraid they would only go further and further astray. After hearing how they had made gods of themselves, the Master exclaimed, This is exactly what I feared most!

Pitying them, the Master decided that he would go to the nation himself. Perhaps he could lead them away from their folly.

So the Master went. He came to the guards who had been stationed around each peak. These guards were presumably of more humble rank since they had to stand below in the foul air of the earth. Anyone who had a higher rank would never deign to associate with the rest of the world lest they be contaminated, nor would they ever converse with those below, lest they be polluted by the noxious vapours emanating from their lowly mouths. Thus the guards who were stationed below the city were most certainly of the humble folk. Yet they still clung to the icons of their gods and were always embracing and kissing them, since they, too, maintained that the essence of their faith was money.

The Master approached one of the guards and began to discuss the purpose of life with him—how the true point of living is to devote oneself to divine worship, the Holy Law, prayer and virtuous deeds. Money is pure folly, he said, and not the purpose of life. The guard did not heed him at all. It had been firmly established long ago that the most important thing in life was money.

When the Master came to another guard and began speaking with him, this guard would not listen either. And it was much the same with all the rest of the guards; they all refused to hear the Master's words. So the Master decided to go into the city, which was located atop the mountain peak. How he was able to enter the city was a source of wonderment, and the people there asked him, How did you get here? No outsider has ever been able to set foot here!

He answered, Why ask? After all, I got here, did I not?

The Master then began to discuss the purpose of life with one of the city's denizens, saying that money was in no way life's purpose, as he had said before to the guards. The man paid no heed to the Master, nor did anyone else, as they all were so deluded in their folly that they would listen to no one. But the people were all astonished by the arrival of a stranger in their city who had been able to enter and who spoke to them in a fashion so counter to their faith. They suspected that this man must be the Master of Prayer. News of someone called the pious Master of Prayer had been widespread throughout the world. But no one was ever able to apprehend him because each time he appeared in a different guise: to one he might appear to be a merchant and to another a pauper.

Then, he promptly absconded from the city.

And it came to pass...

There was a mighty and valiant Warrior who had gathered together a number of other warriors. This Warrior, together with his fellow warriors, set out conquering countries. The Warrior only wished for countries to submit to his rule. If they simply surrendered to him, then he would leave them in peace. But if they did not, he would bring that country to ruin. So he went about, conquering various countries. He had no desire for wealth; his only wish was submission. The Warrior's custom was to remain at a distance of fifty miles and dispatch his warriors into a country to demand its surrender. Just so, he conquered more and more countries.

The merchants of the Nation of Wealth who conducted their business abroad returned home and told what they had heard of the mighty Warrior. A great panic ensued. Even though they would have readily surrendered, they had heard that he abhorred money and wanted none of it, which was obviously sheer blasphemy. So they could not simply surrender to him, for that would be tantamount to abandoning their faith. Yet they were terribly afraid of the Warrior. So they turned to their rituals of worship, making sacrifices to their gods—that is, to their countrymen who had the most money. They would take a beast—one of those having less money, whom they considered subhuman—and offer him as a sacrifice to their gods.

Yet the mighty Warrior continued his advance towards them. He sent forth his other warriors to ask the nation's citizens how they wished to proceed, as was his custom. The people of the nation were terrified and did not know what to do. The merchants had a suggestion: they had visited another country that was populated entirely by gods. There, they said, these gods all rode with angels. This was on account of the fact that in that country everyone, from the humblest to the greatest, was extraordinarily wealthy. Even the least among them would be considered a god according to their foolish misbelief, since even the poorest person there was so rich and possessed enough money to be deemed divine in their own nation. They were said to ride with angels because their horses were adorned opulently with gold and the like, so much so that the value of the horses' caparisons was enough to be deemed an angel by their measure. Some of these gods even rode astride three such angels yoked together.

Therefore, the merchants decided, we should send for help from this country and they will surely aid us since they are all gods.

This suggestion very much pleased everyone as they believed that the divine inhabitants of that country would certainly come to their aid.

Meanwhile, the Master had decided to return once more to the Nation of Wealth. Perhaps, he thought, he could at last steer them away from their persistent folly. So he went. When he came to the guards, he began to converse with one of them, as he was wont to do. This guard told him the news of the mighty Warrior and how everyone was terrified of him.

What do you plan to do? the Master asked the guard.

The guard told him about the plan to send for help from the country where everyone was a god.

The Master laughed heartily at him, saying, What utter foolishness that is! The people there are simply people, just like any of us. You, with your so-called gods, are also just people—nary a one of you is a god. There is but one God in the universe, the One who created all things. Him alone should you serve and to Him you should offer your prayers. This and only this is the true purpose of the world.

The Master told the guard many other things as well. But the guard still would not listen, for folly had long ago taken hold of the people. So the Master continued to press his case with the guard until, at last, the guard responded, Well then, what can I do? I am only one man. There are a great many others in this nation and they far outnumber me.

The guard's response gave some hope that he might yet be turned around from his wayward path. Indeed, the words the Master had spoken when he first met the guard joined with those that he had just said and together they stirred the guard's heart. So the Master went to the next guard and spoke with him, as was his wont. After listening to the Master, this guard responded just as the previous one had. And so, too, all the guards responded in kind.

Afterwards, the Master went into the city and, again, began to converse with people there, as he had before, elucidating the error of their ways—explaining that money was not the main point of living but, rather, that one's true purpose was to be devoted to divine worship, the Holy Law, prayer and so forth. Again, he was ignored, since their infatuation with money had long ago taken hold. But they told him the news of the mighty Warrior and of their plans to send for aid from the country of gods.

Again, the Master scoffed and said that this was pure folly. He told them how these were regular people and they would not be able to help them.

Indeed they are human beings, he told them, just as you are, and they are not gods at all. There is but one God, blessed be He. And as for this mighty Warrior, he wondered aloud, could this be the same Warrior I once knew?

Nobody understood what he meant by this.

So the Master went on his way, talking with one person and then the next, just as he had before. Each time the mighty Warrior was mentioned, he remarked, Could this be the same Warrior...? And each time, no one knew what he meant.

Meanwhile, an uproar had broken out in the city. It was said that there was someone in town going around deriding their faith and saying that there is but the One and Only God, Blessed and Almighty, and every time one speaks of the mighty Warrior he remarks, Could this be the same Warrior I once knew? The people realized that this must be the Master of Prayer, since he was already quite renowned. It was ordered that the Master be found and captured. Even though he always appeared in a different guise, by now they knew all about his shifting disguises. The Master was pursued until at last they apprehended him and he was taken before their elders.

They began to speak with him, and he said much the same as he had told the others before: how they were all living in error and in great folly; how money was not the point of living; how there was the One and Only Blessed God, the Almighty Lord, who created all living things and alone should be worshipped. Money, he told them, was pure folly, and this country that you believe to be populated by gods will never be able to help you since they are just ordinary people and not gods at all.

The elders thought him mad. The whole nation was so steeped in their belief in money and so woefully deluded that anyone who said anything counter to their folly was considered a madman. They asked him, When you speak of the mighty Warrior, why do you always wonder, Could this be the same one?

He answered, Because I once served a great King, and this King's mighty Warrior was lost. So, if this is the same Warrior, I am well acquainted with him. Still, if you are counting on assistance from the country where you believe all to be gods, you are sorely mistaken, for they cannot help you. Rather, putting your trust in them would be your ultimate downfall.

How are you so certain that this would be our downfall? they asked.

He answered, Because the King I served had possession of the Yad, the Guiding Hand. It was a model of a hand, with a palm and five fingers, and scored with all the lines and creases of a human hand. The Yad was a map of all the worlds. And everything that had ever been—since the creation of the heavens and the earth, from the beginning until the very end—and all that was still to be was inscribed in the lines and creases of the hand. The design of all worlds and where each world was situated was indicated precisely on the Yad, just as it would be etched on parchment by the finest cartographer. Every city and every country, every bridge, as well as every forest and every stream, each was marked to note what it was, whether a town or country or the like, and so inscribed on the Yad. Just as on a map, where there are signs and symbols that indicate what each object illustrated upon it represents and explains what is what and how to distinguish a city from a stream and so forth, so there were such signs and symbols in the lines and creases of the Yad. So, too, with all the people who inhabited every country and all the events of their lives. For each and every life was inscribed upon the Yad. All paths from one country to another were there, too, and from one place to the next. That is how I knew how to enter your city, which no one else had ever done before. And should you send me to any other city, I would know the way, for I know the Yad.

Just so, the Yad shows the way from one world into the next. For there is a path that, if followed, leads from this earth into the heavens. No one may ascend without knowing the way, but the Yad shows the way. On the Yad are all the many pathways that lead from one world into the next: the Prophet Elijah ascended to the heavens using one such path, and our teacher Moses ascended using another. So, too, Enoch ascended yet another path after his three hundred and sixty-five years, and that path was inscribed upon the Yad. Thus, each path from one world to another, above and beyond, is marked in the lines and creases of the Yad.

Inscribed upon the Yad is every single thing—as it was at the moment the world came into being up until the present and hereafter. For example, the city of Sodom. The Yad shows how the city was before its destruction, how it was as it was destroyed, and how Sodom appears now, after its ruin. Indeed, all that ever was, is and will be is inscribed upon it. There, on that very Yad, I have seen the country that you believe to be inhabited by gods, and I have seen all its people, who you believe will come to your rescue. This country together, with all its people, will be laid waste.

All this the Master told the elders and all were utterly astonished, for they realized that he had spoken the truth. Indeed, it
was well known that there existed such a map upon which all
things were inscribed. They understood that his words were true
and that such things could not be simply made up. For all were
aware that in the assemblage of lines and creases of this Yad lay
portentous signs and symbols.

They asked him, Where might your great King be? Perhaps
he can show us a path to find more riches?

He shot back in surprise and anger, You still want money?
Speak no more of it!

They persisted, Nevertheless, tell us where your King is.

He answered, I myself do not know where he is. Here is the
story as to why:

Once there was a King and a Queen who had an only daughter. When the time came for a marriage to be arranged for her,
all the royal counsellors were assembled to advise to whom she
should be wed. I was among them, since I was much loved by the
King. I suggested that she be given to the King's mighty Warrior.
As he had done numerous favours for us by conquering many
countries, it would be fitting to give him the Princess as a bride.
My suggestion delighted the King and all agreed. There was a
great celebration as a husband had been found for the Princess.

The Princess and the Warrior were married and the Princess
had a Child. The Child was an extraordinarily magnificent
being, possessing preternatural beauty. His hair was golden and
glittered with an array of colours. His face beamed like the sun
and his eyes like brilliant celestial lights. He was born with an

innate wisdom, and right from his birth it was evident that he was already a great sage. When anyone said something witty, he knew to laugh. In other cases, too, he proved to be a great savant, even if he was not yet able to comport himself like an adult, lacking as he did the ability to speak and the like. But it was immediately evident to all that he was brilliant.

The King had an Orator, who was a master of rhetoric and eloquence. He declaimed fine speeches and very lovely poetry and paeans for the King. Although this Orator was already very eloquent, the King showed him a path: the way to obtain exceptional power in the science of oratory. Following this way, he became the most wonderful Orator.

Moreover, the King had a Sage. The King showed him a path, too: the way to obtain even greater wisdom. Following this way, he became the most exceedingly marvellous Sage.

The mighty Warrior was, likewise, an accomplished soldier in his own right. But the King showed him a path to obtain great might. Following this way, he became the most extraordinary and magnificent Warrior.

Now, there was a sword, suspended in the air. This sword had three powers: when it was held high, all the battle chiefs would flee and all enemies at war would thereby be easily laid waste. With the chiefs having fled, their enemies would be left with no one to lead them in battle and would be routed. Yet, there might remain some who continued to wage war. However, the sword was double-bladed and each blade had its own unique power. The swing of one blade brought instant death, while the other delivered a wasting disease to its foes, making them wither and their flesh shrivel, as is the nature of a plague, heaven protect us. With but a swing of the sword, all enemies are struck down by either sudden death or protracted disease, according to each blade's power. The King showed the Warrior his path and, along with it, this sword. By this way he obtained his great might.

The King showed me the path to obtain my own craft, too. From this path I received all that I needed to further my way of prayer.

The King also had a Favourite, who was much beloved by him and who loved him greatly in return. So much so, in fact, that they could not spend even an hour outside the other's company. Yet, since there are times when they had to be apart, they had portraits painted of the two of them together. They would take delight in the portraits whenever they could not see one another in the flesh. These depicted the King and his Favourite loving each other, as they kissed and embraced with great amorousness. The portraits had a special quality that whoever beheld them was overwhelmed by a feeling of deep affection. The King's Favourite obtained his profound love following a path that the King had shown him.

The time came when all of us—including the Orator, the mighty Warrior and the other members of the King's retinue—went to the places where we received the powers that furthered each of our crafts. Each followed his own path in order to restore his strength.

And it came to pass...

A great gale arose in the world and confounded all in its wake. The sea was overturned onto dry land and the dry land became as the sea. Wastelands became fertile plains and fertile plains became wastelands. The entire world was turned upside down. The gale blew into the King's chambers. There it did no damage, but it seized hold of the Princess's Child. Amidst the hurly-burly that immediately followed the snatching of her dear Child, the Princess raced after to get him back and she, too, disappeared— whither, no one knew.

So, too, went the Queen, and after her, the King. Each went chasing after the Child until, at last, they were scattered over the face of the earth. No one knew where they were, for none of us was there. We had been at the places where our powers were to be restored, and when we returned, everyone was gone. The Yad, too, had gone missing.

From that moment on, all of us were scattered over the earth, no longer able to find the places to restore our powers as every-thing had been overturned. We had to seek new paths now, since we could not make our way to the particular places whence each had once drawn his strength. Yet the vestiges of that strength remain strong from long ago. If this Warrior, whom you fear so, is the King's Warrior, then he is a very mighty warrior indeed.

Thus the Master said to the gathered elders and they were astonished as they listened. The elders compelled the Master to stay and would not allow him to leave, lest the Warrior came to attack, for the Master knew the Warrior well from their time in the King's retinue.

The mighty Warrior continued his advance towards the Nation of Wealth and to dispatch his messengers as he approached. He encamped below the city and sent his messengers in to learn whether or not the country would surrender. The people were terribly afraid and they asked the Master for his advice. The Master told them that it was necessary for him to observe the manner of this warrior to see if he could recognize whether it was the King's Warrior.

So the Master went out to meet the Warrior. He approached his armed guards and began speaking with one of the Warrior's accompanying warriors in order to ascertain whether this was the mighty Warrior he once knew. The Master asked, What is it that you do and how is it that you came to be with this mighty Warrior? The Warrior's warrior answered, This is the tale that took place:

As it is written in the chronicles, there was a great tempest and this tempest turned the entire world upside down. The sea was overturned onto dry land and the dry land became as the sea. Wastelands became fertile plains and the fertile plains became wastelands. Everything was all mixed up. When all the upheaval was done, the whole world was topsy-turvy. So the people decided that they needed to appoint a new king to rule. They deliberated about who would be fit to be their king and they recognized that the principal matter to consider is the true meaning of life. Whosoever is most devoted to this and applies himself to the ultimate goal of life should be their king. But they got to thinking, What, then, is the ultimate purpose of living? And among them were several opinions.

Some said that the central purpose could only be honour, for it is clear that honour is essential in this world. If a man is disrespected, that is, when dishonourable things are said against him, this leads to bloodshed. So you see, honour is essential for the whole world in that even after death one's honour is still preserved, conferring respect to the dead and burying him with reverence and the like, all while declaring that such ceremony is performed on your behalf and for your honour. For although the dead no longer have need of money or surely anything else for that matter, yet one continues to revere the dead and do all one can to preserve their honour. So, certainly, the main and central principle in the whole world is honour.

Further suppositions and arguments were brought forth, all asserting the premise that honour is the main purpose and principle of all. At last, some concluded this was so and, to that end, they resolved to find a revered and esteemed man, one who also demanded ever more respect and honour. For a highly venerated man seeking even more honour only furthers the propensity for honour in the world and demonstrates that his sole purpose is this fundamental principle and its attainment. Therefore, such a man deserves to be king.

Such was the foolish view held by a group of them, based on such absurd reasoning, and it led them far astray. For this group, honour and respect were the central purpose, while other factions, based on their own foolish ideas, made all sorts of other conclusions.

So this group went searching for such a man. They went out and saw an old Gypsy beggar being carried aloft, followed by nearly five hundred other Gypsies. The old beggar was blind and mute and hunchbacked. Those who trailed behind him were all part of his evil brood, his sisters and brothers, and their wicked offspring, who came to number this many. All of them followed him and carried him on the way, taking great care to show their respect for this old beggar even though he sneered at them and bitterly cursed them all the while as he ordered one and then another to carry him, continually heaping scorn upon them.

Thus the group in search of an honoured and venerated king determined that this old beggar was a highly esteemed and respected man. Indeed, he had clearly attained great honour and yet sought even more and was steadfast in further acquiring it. They were pleased by this beggar and took him for their king.

Now, the land itself must be amenable. There must be an amenable land that is most conducive for respect to flourish just as another may be more conducive for other purposes. So the group that held honour as the ultimate goal sought a land most amenable and conducive for veneration. When they found a land most fitting, they settled there.

Others held that honour was not the main purpose, for they considered murderousness to be the essential principle of the world and its chief quality. For as we can see, all things that exist in the world are subject to destruction. Everything in the world—from the grass and crops to human beings—eventually must cease. Accordingly, the essence of all things is that they are bound to end. Thus, a killer, who slays and destroys people, advances the world towards its final end. The chief quality of this world, they decided, is murderousness. So they sought a murderer, full of fury and malice, who they, in their deluded way, believed was truer to the ultimate purpose and deserved to be king.

As they went searching for such a man, they heard a cry. When they asked what this cry was, they were told that it was someone who had just slaughtered his father and mother.

Where, they thought, could you find a more stone-hearted murderer? Who could be more savage than he who has slain his own father and mother? This man has attained the ultimate goal. They were very pleased by this killer and took him for their king.

They sought a land that would be most amenable for murderousness and decided on a place in the mountains where murderers were known to hole up. There they went to settle with their new king.

Some said that the one who is most fit to be king is he who has an abundance to eat but does not consume the food of common men, but rather only the most refined things (such as milk, which does not corrupt the intellect). Although they reckoned that such a man deserves to be king, they could not straight away find such a person who did not consume the food of common men. In the meantime, they chose a rich man who had a great deal of food and a highly refined palate to serve as their interim king until they could find the man they truly wanted. So, for the time being, they chose the rich man for their king and found a suitable land. There they settled.

Some said that a beautiful woman ought to rule them. The chief goal of the world is that it be inhabited—indeed, for that very purpose it was created! As beauty arouses desire, thereby the population increases. Accordingly, a beautiful woman helps advance this ultimate goal of the world and one who possesses beauty ought to be our ruler. So they found an exceptionally beautiful woman and she was made their ruler. Then, they searched and found a land most fitting where they settled.

Some said that the most essential thing in the world was the power of speech, for that is what distinguishes man from beast. Eloquence is the chief thing that marks a person as greater than an animal. Accordingly, this is truly the essential quality and we should seek someone with the gift of the gab, a polyglot, well spoken in the world's languages, who should be able to hold forth all the time. Such a man is on the path to attaining the ultimate goal. They went and found a mad Frenchman, who was wandering about and talking to himself. They asked if he knew languages and he knew several. In their deluded view, such a man had certainly attained that which was most indispensable. Indeed, he was quite a raconteur and apparently conversant in many tongues, and he sure could talk a lot, even to himself. So they were very pleased by him and took him for their king. They chose a land that was most amenable and there they went to settle with their new king, for he would certainly set them on the right path.

Some said that the essential goal in life is pleasure. For when a child is born there is great merriment, and at a wedding it is very gay indeed. And there is great happiness, too, when a nation is victorious in its conquests. Accordingly, the most fundamental thing of all is pleasure. So they went looking for a man who was always happy, since he is on the path to attaining the ultimate goal in the world and he ought to be their king. They went and found a Ukrainian peasant ambling along in a filthy shirt and carrying a bottle of liquor. A large group of peasants were trailing behind him. This peasant was very happy because he was quite drunk. They saw that he was full of mirth and had not a care in the world. They were well pleased with him because he was on the path to attaining the ultimate goal, which was happiness, so took him to be their king. Undoubtedly he would lead them on the righteous path. They chose a land that was most amenable, that is, where there were vineyards for making wine and grappa from the grape seeds. No part of the grapes should go to waste, because, for them, the essential quality was for people to drink and get drunk and be forever merry. Even though there were no grounds for their happiness, as they had nothing to be happy about, their essential goal was nevertheless to indulge always in pleasure. So they chose a land amenable to that and there they went and settled.

Some said that the essence of life is wisdom, so they went looking for a great sage and made him their king. They sought out a land amenable to wisdom and went and settled there.

Some said that the essential goal is to devote oneself to taking food and drink for the purpose of enlarging one's limbs. So they looked for a stout-limbed man who spent his time strengthening and growing his body. He who has large limbs has a greater share in the world, as he occupies more space in it. That man was closer to the essential goal since the essential goal was the enlargement of the limbs. Accordingly, such a man was fit to be king. They went and found a towering Hungarian whom they were pleased with because he was so stout-limbed and thus on the path to attaining the ultimate goal and they made him king. They sought out a land amenable to this essential goal and went and settled there.

A troop of this kingdom's stout-limbed soldiers sallied forth with a convoy of wagons carrying their food, drink and other supplies.

The world naturally cowered before these stout-limbed soldiers for they were large men and warriors. Whoever encountered them withdrew at once.

While this troop was making their way, they encountered a great Warrior. This Warrior did not back away from the soldiers, instead he rushed headlong into them, scattering them this way and that. The men of the troop feared him. He went among the wagons of the convoy and ate up everything in sight. To the soldiers it was terribly bewildering and they instantly fell down before him. *Long live the king!* they cried, making him at once their king, for he was clearly entitled to be their ruler. To their way of thinking, the essential quality was being stout-limbed. The current king readily yielded his kingship, for this Warrior was clearly entitled to the throne, being such a great warrior and so stout-limbed. And so it was. They made this warrior their king.

And that is the Warrior, the soldier continued, whom we are now accompanying to conquer the world. But this Warrior does not plan to rule the world by his conquest. Rather, he seems to have a different purpose entirely.

All this one of the Warrior's warriors told the Master when he asked how he had come to be with the Warrior.

But there was yet another group who said that none of the other things were the essential goal. The true essential purpose of living is to devote oneself in prayer to Blessed God, and to be meek and humble. They looked for a Master of Prayer and made him their king. (To be sure, all the other groups were in error, misled into folly—each led into its own folly by its foolish opinions and witless suppositions. This last group, however, had hit upon the truth, and good for them!)

And it came to pass...

The Master asked another of the Warrior's warriors, What is the nature of the valour of the Warrior who is now your king?

He replied, When a country does not wish to submit to him, then our Warrior unsheathes his sword, a sword with three distinct powers. When it is raised aloft, all the officers flee...

As soon as the Master heard this, he realized that this was surely the King's Warrior. So the Master asked if it were possible to arrange a meeting with the Warrior. The soldier replied, He must be informed.

So the soldier went and informed the Warrior, who ordered that the Master be admitted. When the Master entered, they recognized one another and there was great joy at the boon of their chance meeting. There was great happiness, but also tears, as they remembered the King and his retinue.

The Master and the Warrior began to chat about how they had both arrived there. The Warrior recalled to the Master how they were all scattered after the great tempest had struck. When he made his way back from the place he had gone to regain his strength, he found neither King nor retinue. So he set off and, as he wandered, discovered various traces where he recognized that the King and his retinue had been. Standing at one such spot, he realized that the King had certainly been there but he could find neither hide nor hair of him. Similarly, he passed another place where he recognized the Queen surely had been, but he could find no trace of her either. In this way he discovered places that the King's retinue had been. Of you, however, he said to the Master, I never found a trace.

The Master replied, I discovered all the places the retinue had been, including you. Once I passed a place where I saw the King's crown, and I realized that the King had most certainly been there. But I, too, could find neither hide nor hair of him, so I continued on my way. Then I came to a sea of blood, which I gathered must surely have come from the tears the Queen shed and I recognized that our Queen had surely been there. But I could find neither hair nor hide of her. I then came to a sea of milk, which I understood must surely have come from the milk of the Princess whose Child was lost. She expressed her milk, which became this sea of milk. The Princess had surely been there, but I could find neither hair nor hide of her. I continued on and spied the golden hair of the Child lying on the ground. I did not dare take any of it. I knew that surely the Child had been there, but of him I found no trace.

Continuing on my way I came upon a sea of wine. I knew that this sea had surely flowed from the speech of the Orator who must have let loose a stream of words of consolation for the King and the Queen. Then he turned and streamed forth words of consolation for the Princess. And these streams joined to become the sea of wine. But I could not find him, so I went on my way. I saw a stone on which was engraved the same diagrams that were on the Yad. I understood from this that the King's Sage had surely been here and had engraved the image of the Yad upon the stone. But it was impossible to find him.

So onward I went and saw exhibited upon a mountain the golden tablecloths and credenzas and all the King's treasures. From this I gleaned that the King's Chamberlain had surely been here, too, but it was impossible to find him.

The Master finished speaking and the Warrior responded, I too passed by all those places. Indeed, I did take some of our Child's golden hair. I took seven hairs of various hues. They are very precious to me. I sat and took delight in what I could, such as the grass and the beauties of nature until there was nothing left to delight in. Then I set off again, and when I left that place I forgot my bow there.

The Master interjected, I saw your bow. I knew that it was surely yours, but I could not find you.

The Warrior continued, When I left that place I walked on until I encountered a troop of warriors. I wandered among them, for I was very hungry and wanted to eat. As soon as I had intruded on them they instantly made me their king. Now I am going about conquering the world. But my true intention is to find our King and his retinue.

The Master inquired of the Warrior what ought to be done about the people of the Nation of Wealth who were so deceived into the lust for money that they ended up with such absurd ideas.

The Warrior answered that he had heard from the King that one can be extricated from all desires, but the one who has fallen into the lust for money can never be so extricated.

So you will never prevail upon them, he said, because it is impossible to extricate them. That said, I also once heard from the King that, indeed, one might be able to free them from the lust for money by following the path towards the sword whence I derive my valour.

The Warrior and the Master sat together for a while. Remembering the elders who had asked the Master to speak to the Warrior on their behalf, the Master prevailed upon the Warrior to extend his ultimatum before which they would not be harmed, and the Warrior agreed. The two of them established signals by which one might get news from the other. Then, the Master left to continue on his way.

As the Master walked back, he noticed a group of people entreating Blessed God and praying while carrying prayer books. He was as startled by them as they were by him. He stood and prayed, and they stood and prayed as well. He then asked them, Who are you?

They replied, When the tempest struck, the world was divided into many different groups. Some people chose one group, while others chose another. We decided that the essential goal in life is only to devote oneself eternally to prayer to Blessed God. We searched and found a master of prayer, and we made him our king.

When the Master heard this he was very pleased because that was his sole desire, too. So he started to converse with them, showing them his orders of prayers, his prayer books and his other accoutrements of prayer. When they heard what he had to say their eyes goggled and they saw the greatness of the Master. They instantly made him their king. Their erstwhile king relinquished his kingship to him for they saw he was a great man. The Master studied with them and opened their eyes and showed them how to pray to Blessed God. He turned them into great and utter tzaddikim. They had been tzaddikim before, for they had been solely devoted to prayer. But the Master opened their eyes to allow them to become great tzaddikim. The Master sent a letter to the Warrior, informing him that he had the honour of finding such people as he had wanted and had become their new king.

Meanwhile, the Nation of Wealth continued engaging in their affairs and in their mad forms of worship, sacrificing to their gods (who were wealthy people) and the like. The ultimatum that the Warrior had set was rapidly approaching and they were very frightened. They performed their religious rites and offered sacrifices and burned incense and busied themselves with their prayers to their gods. They seized a minor beast—namely a person who had less money—and offered him as a sacrifice. They remained of the opinion that they had to follow the original piece of advice that was offered to them, to appeal to the country where everyone was a god. That country would surely help them because they were all gods. Thus they did and sent emissaries to that country.

As the emissaries were on their way, they got lost. They spied a man walking along whose walking stick was of greater value than all their gods combined, inlaid as it was with very expensive jewels, making it exceed the wealth of all their gods put together. If you took the wealth of all their gods and even the gods of the country to which they were headed, that stick was still worth more than all their wealth. The man was wearing a bejewelled cap, also worth an immense amount of money. When the emissaries saw the man they instantly fell to the ground, making prostrations and obeisance, because in their misguided belief they held this man to be a god above all other gods. This man whom they had encountered was the King's Chamberlain.

The man said to them, You think this is remarkable? Come with me and I will show you some true riches.

He led them up the mountain where the King's treasure was laid out and showed it all to them. When they saw it they instantly fell to the ground, making prostrations and obeisance, for he was a god above all their other gods. But they offered no sacrifice. While according to their misguided opinion he was a god supreme, and they would surely have offered sacrifices to him, the emissaries had been instructed not to offer any sacrifices on the road because they were afraid that should they do so none of them would remain in the end. The reason being that if one of them should find a treasure on the road, or if another should go into a privy and find a treasure there, they each might sacrifice each of themselves unto the newfound gods, one by one, until none of them would remain.

The emissaries considered why they should be going to the country of the gods whither they had been dispatched. Instead, this man might better be able to help them because he was a god above all of them (according to their insane opinion) since he had an immensely greater amount of wealth than the others. So they asked the man whether he would accompany them to their country. He agreed and went along with them. They arrived in their country and there was much rejoicing at receiving such a god. They felt assured that through him assistance would surely be rendered. He was after all a great god, as he had such great wealth.

The Chamberlain decreed that no more sacrifices were to be offered until his rule of law was established in the land. The Chamberlain clearly abhorred the foolish customs of the Nation of Wealth. But he still could not deter them from their wicked path. He did, however, order that no more sacrifices be offered.

The people of the nation started asking him about how they should deal with the Warrior, of whom they were so afraid. The Chamberlain answered them, wondering whether it was the same Warrior that he knew. So the Chamberlain rose and went down to meet the Warrior. He asked the Warrior's entourage if it were possible to have an audience with him. They said they would announce him. They did so, and the Warrior ordered him to be let in. The Chamberlain went in to see the Warrior, and they instantly recognized one another. There was great happiness and tears.

The Warrior said to the Chamberlain, Our virtuous Master of Prayer has also been here. I have already seen him. He has become a king, too.

The Chamberlain then related that he had discovered all the places everyone had been, including that of the King and his retinue. But he had never come across places where the Master and the Warrior had been. He and the Warrior discussed the nation where they were so deluded and seduced by money as to fall into such folly.

The Warrior replied with what he had told the Master. He had heard from the King that whoever fell into the lust for money could never be extricated except, perhaps, by finding the path to the aforementioned sword. The two of them discussed this at length, but the Chamberlain prevailed upon the Warrior to extend the ultimatum for the nation, which he did. Then they established signals by which one might get news from the other.

The Chamberlain then left the Warrior and returned to the Nation of Wealth. The Chamberlain severely reproached the citizens there for the evil path they had strayed upon with regard to money. But he could not lead them from it for they were so deeply entrenched in it. Nevertheless, since the Master and the Chamberlain devoted so much time to holding forth about it, the people had become a bit perplexed. Even though they still clung to their deluded opinion and did not want to be extricated from their folly, at last they said, Alright already, lead us out of it. If it is indeed the case that we are in error, lead us out of our folly.

The Chamberlain said to the people there, I shall give you some advice regarding the Warrior, for I know his power and whence he derives his valour.

He went on to tell them of the sword, which was the source of the Warrior's strength.

So I shall accompany you on the way to the sword and through it you shall be the equal of the Warrior, deriving the same strength from it as he does.

The Chamberlain's true intent was for the people to find the path to the sword, which would lead them out of their lust for money, since that path to the sword might lead them out of such lust.

The people accepted his advice and dispatched their great leaders, that is to say, their gods, to accompany the Chamberlain on the path to the sword. To accompany the Chamberlain, these gods dressed themselves for the journey in vestments adorned with gold and silver, for that was the most important thing to them. They all headed off together, the Chamberlain and the country's great divine leaders.

The Chamberlain informed the Warrior of the fact that he was leading them on the path to the sword, hoping that along the way they might have the privilege of finding the King and his retinue.

The Warrior said, I will join you on your way.

So the people accompanying the Chamberlain would not recognize him as the Warrior, he disguised himself and went with them. The Chamberlain and the Warrior decided to inform the Master, and the Master said he would also join them. Before he left, the Master told his people to pray to Blessed God that their way might be successful and that they might be deemed worthy of finding the King and his retinue. The Master would always pray thus for the recovery of the King and his retinue and would always command his people to pray accordingly. He composed prayers for them to offer. Now that he was off on the journey to find the King and his retinue, he told them to pray even more steadfastly than ever in his absence that he and his companions be worthy of finding them.

When the Master joined the Chamberlain and the Warrior there was certainly great rejoicing, with happiness and tears. The three went on together, along with the country's gods. They travelled on and on and arrived in a country where guards were stationed at its border.

They asked the guards, What country is this and who is your king?

The guards replied, When the great tempest struck, and the world was divided into many groups, the people of this country chose wisdom as their principal goal and accepted a great sage as their king. It was not long before they had found an immensely great sage who was uniquely and exceedingly wise. The erstwhile king relinquished his kingship to him and they made this sage their new king, for their principal ideal was wisdom.

The Chamberlain, the Warrior and the Master said, Clearly this must be our Sage.

The three asked whether it were possible to obtain an audience with their king. The guards replied that they would announce them. They did so, and he ordered they be let in. The three went in to see the sage who had become king of that country and they all instantly recognized one another, for this sage was indeed the King's Sage. There was, of course, great rejoicing, with happiness and tears. They cried over not finding the King and the rest of his retinue.

They asked the Sage whether he knew of the King's Yad. He replied that he had the Yad, but since they had been dispersed by the great tempest he had no wish to look into it, as it belonged to the King alone. But he had engraved the image of the Yad on a stone so it might be useful to his work. But he had never looked into the original Yad again.

They chatted with the Sage about how he had come to be there and he told them that after the great tempest he went wherever his feet took him. On his travels he passed by every place except those where the Master, the Warrior and the Chamberlain had been. Eventually the people of this country found him and made him their king. For the time being he had to lead them according to their practice and their wisdom until he could lead them forth into the real truth.

They discussed with the Sage the Nation of Wealth where the people had become so deluded into the lust for money.

The others said, If only we were no longer so scattered and dispersed. For that nation's sake, it would indeed be a great boon to correct their ways and turn them to the truth, for they have been so misled. Indeed, each one of the groups chose its own folly; some chose honour, some chose murderousness, and so forth, and were all thereby deluded. All of them need to be led forth towards the true goal. For even the group that chose for itself the goal of wisdom has not reached the true goal. They, too, need to be led forth, because they adhere to profane knowledge and slip into apostasy. It is far easier, however, to extricate people from other follies. Those who have been deluded into the idolatry of money, and have fallen into it so deeply, cannot be extricated.

The Sage replied that he, too, had heard from the King that one could be extricated from all the lusts, but from the lust for money one could not be extricated except by means of the path to the mighty sword. The Sage said that he would also accompany them, and the four of them continued on their way together, along with the so-called gods who were with them.

They came to another country and asked the guards stationed there, What country is this and who is your king?

The guards replied, When the great tempest struck, the people of this country chose eloquence as the most essential thing and decided to have a masterful orator as their king. So they found a great grandiloquent master of rhetoric and made him their king. The erstwhile king relinquished his kingship to him for he saw this was a true master of rhetoric.

The four surmised, That must surely be our King's Orator.

They asked if it were possible to have an audience with their king. They said they would announce him. They did so, and the king ordered them to be let in. They went in to see the king, and it was indeed the King's Orator. They all instantly recognized one another. There was great happiness and tears.

The Orator decided to accompany them as they continued on their search to find the rest, for they saw that Blessed God was helping them find their companions. This they attributed to the merit of their virtuous Master of Prayer, who was always praying for their reunion. Through the intercession of the Master's prayers they were deemed worthy of finding their companions. So they continued on in the hope of finding the rest.

They travelled on and came to the border of another country and asked the guards, What country is this and who is your king?

The guards replied that they were of the group that had chosen pleasure and carousal as their chief goal. They had made a drunkard their king for he was always happy. Not long after, they came upon a man who was sitting in a sea of wine. He pleased them far more because he was surely a very great drunkard indeed, sitting as he was in a whole sea of wine. They took him for their new king.

The five asked whether they might have an audience with their king. The guards went and announced them. When they were let in to see him, they saw that this was, indeed, the King's

Favourite, who had been sitting in the sea of wine, which had come from the Orator's words of consolation. When they went in to see him they all instantly recognized one another, and there was great happiness and tears. The Favourite joined and went along with them.

They travelled on and came to another country. They asked the guards, Who is your king?

They replied that their monarch was a beautiful woman, because she advanced their ultimate goal, which was the populating of the world. Previously they had had a beautiful woman to rule over them, but then they found a woman of truly exceptional beauty. They made her their new ruler.

They surmised, That must surely be the Princess.

The six asked whether they might have an audience with her. The guards went and announced them, and they were let in to see this queen. They instantly recognized her as the Princess and the rejoicing that resulted was beyond description.

They asked, How did you come to be here?

She described how when the great tempest struck and snatched her dear Child from its crib, in that moment of chaos she ran after her Child but could not find it. She expressed her milk and it became a sea of milk. Afterwards she found this country and they made her their ruler. There was much rejoicing as well as a great deal of crying over the precious Child who was not there, and over her father and mother whose whereabouts she did not know. At last, her country had a king, too, for the mighty Warrior—the husband of the Princess (who was now this country's ruler)—was now by her side.

The Princess entreated the Master to go into her country and cleanse it of its shameful vice. Among them, the ultimate goal was beauty and they were demoralized by their carnal lust. Accordingly, she asked the Master if he could cleanse them of it and exhort them not to wallow in their lascivious lust nor act so crudely in that vice. For this unseemly lust was an article of faith among them.

Out they set to search for the rest. Travelling on, they arrived at another country where they asked, Who is your king?

The border guards answered that their king was a yearling child. They were of the group that had decided that the one who should be their king was he who had a great deal of nourishment but did not feed on the food of common people. They had had a wealthy man as their king, but they later found a person who was sitting in a sea of milk. He pleased them greatly since he nourished himself, living on milk, and did not feed on the food of other people. Accordingly, they made him their king. And that was why they called him the yearling king, because he lived on milk like a one-year-old.

The seven surmised that this must surely be their Child, so they asked whether they might have an audience with him. The guards went and announced them, and they were let in to see him. They instantly recognized one another; and he recognized them even though he had been a mere babe when he was snatched away, because he was a great savant from the moment of his birth and born with much wisdom. And clearly they recognized him, too. There was understandably a great deal of rejoicing, but also many tears over the missing King and Queen.

They asked him, How did you come to be here?

He described how when the great tempest had struck and snatched him, it had borne him away somewhere. There he sustained himself on what he found around him until he came to the sea of milk. He instantly understood that this sea had surely come from his mother's own milk; she had undoubtedly expressed it and it became that sea. So he sat there in the sea of milk and was nourished by it until the people of the country came and made him their king.

The eight of them continued on their way and came to another country where they asked, Who is your king?

These guards answered that they had chosen murderousness as the essential principle of the world and had made a murderer their king. Then, they found a woman sitting in a sea of blood and made her their monarch, because they saw that she was clearly an even greater murderer, sitting as she was in a sea of blood.

They then asked whether they might have an audience with their monarch. The guards went and announced them, and they were let in to see her. This was the Queen who wept constantly and whose tears had become the sea of blood. They all instantly recognized one another. Unsurprisingly there was much rejoicing, but also many tears over the absence of the King.

The nine continued on their way and came to yet another country where they asked, Who is your king?

They answered that they had chosen as their king an esteemed man, for among them honour was the essential principle of the world. They found an old man sitting in a field with a crown upon his head. He pleased them greatly; he clearly was an esteemed man, sitting as he was in a field with a crown upon his head. So they made him their king.

They surmised that he must surely be their King. So they asked whether it might be possible to have an audience with him. The guards went and announced them, and they were let in to see him. They instantly recognized that this was indeed their King, and the rejoicing that ensued was more than a mind could fathom. For the life of them, the foolish so-called gods from the Nation of Wealth who had trailed along on the journey had no idea what was going on nor why everyone was so happy.

Now the holy community was again reunited: the King and all his holy retinue. They sent the Master to all the countries of the groups that had chosen wicked things as their principal goals in order to reprove them and cleanse them and extricate them from their misguided state. He was to lead them out of their vices and follies for they had all been so deluded. Now the Master surely had the power to turn them round onto the right path. Power and authority had been ceded by the erstwhile kings of all those countries, and all their present kings were now alongside him. So, with the authority of their new kings, the Master went to cleanse the various countrymen of their wayward ways and turn them around towards repentance.

The Warrior spoke with the King concerning the nation that had fallen into idolatry of money. The Warrior said to the King, I have heard from Your Majesty that by means of the path to the sword, one can extricate those who have fallen into the lust for money.

The King replied, Indeed, that is so.

The King told the Warrior that branching from the path to the sword there was a sidetrack that led to a mountain of fire. On that mountain lived a lion. When it needed to eat, it attacked the flocks, taking sheep and livestock and devouring them. The shepherds knew of the lion and tried to protect their sheep from it. But the lion paid no heed. Rather, when it wished to feed, it fell upon the flocks, and the shepherds raised a hue and cry and raged at the lion, but the lion remained heedless and took the sheep and livestock, roaring and devouring them. This mountain of fire was invisible.

Branching from the path to the sword there was another sidetrack leading to a place known as the Kitchen. In the Kitchen all manner of delicacies were made but there was no oven. The foods were cooked by the flames of the lion's fiery mountain, which was quite far away. There were conduits and furrows running from the mountain of fire to the Kitchen by means of which the delicacies were cooked. The Kitchen, too, was invisible. But birds perched atop it were the tell-tale sign as to where the Kitchen was. The birds fanned their wings either to stoke or to weaken the fire. They fanned the flames according to the needs of the food, that is, each food required a different kind of heat.

All this the King told the Warrior. You shall lead the people from the Nation of Wealth, he went on, towards this path—first into the wind so they should catch the scent of the delicacies, and then when you give them some of the food, they will surely be rid of their lust for money.

The Warrior did just that, taking along the great leaders of the country of wealth who had accompanied the Chamberlain

and who, when they left their country, had been given the
authority to do whatever was necessary. The Warrior took those
people and guided them along the path the King had told him
of and brought them into the Kitchen. First he led them into
the wind where they caught the scent of the food. They started
to implore him to give him some of those delicacies. Then he
led them upwind and they started to shout about an exceedingly
fetid odour.

The Warrior said to them, You can see for yourselves there is
nothing here that could make such a stench. Clearly it must be you
who stinks, for there is nothing here that has such a putrid odour.

He then gave them some of the delicacies. As soon as they
ate, they instantly began casting off their gold and silver and
throwing their money away. Each one dug a pit and buried
himself in it because of the great shame they felt so keenly. As
they tasted the food, they knew it was their wealth that reeked
so terribly. They tore at their faces and buried themselves and
could not raise their heads. They all felt such shame. Such was
the nature of the delicacies: whoever ate of them hated money.
In that place, money was the greatest humiliation. Should one of
them wish to insult another he did so by saying, You have money!
Money was a very great shame there, and the more money one
had the more shame he bore. No one could raise his head, even
to look at one another, let alone the Warrior. Whoever found in
his possession a gulden or a groschen would immediately cast it
aside, throwing it far away.

Later, the Warrior came to them and took them out of the
pits in which they had buried themselves out of shame and said

to them, Come with me. Now you need have no further fear of the Warrior, for I am that very Warrior.

They asked the Warrior to give them some of the food so they could take it back to their nation. They themselves would forever abhor money, but they wanted the entire land to be extricated from the lust for it. The Warrior doled out the delicacies, and they brought them back to their nation.

As soon as the people were given the food from the Kitchen, they all instantly began throwing away their money and burying themselves in the ground out of their great shame. The wealthy people and the so-called gods felt the greatest shame, while those who were referred to as beasts and birds were ashamed at even having considered themselves so insignificant because they had less money. For now they finally knew that it was just the opposite: money is the world's principal abomination. The delicacies possessed such a quality that whoever ate of them came to detest money, which now had the rank stench of shit. So without exception they threw away their money, all their gold and all their silver.

Later, they were sent the Master of Prayer, who doled out penance and atonement. He cleansed them, and the King became ruler over the entire world, and the world turned itself around and returned to Blessed God. All devoted themselves to the Holy Law and prayer and repentance and good deeds.

Amen. May it be His will.
Blessed be God forever
Amen and
Amen

THIRTEENTH TALE

Of Seven Beggars

*I shall tell you how
people once were
merry.*

A story:

O NCE THERE WAS a king. The king had an only son to
whom he wished to grant his kingdom while he was
still living. So he threw a great banquet. Now when the king
throws a banquet, it is, of course, a merry affair. Handing over
his kingdom to his son while he was alive was an especially
grand celebration. All the royal ministers attended the banquet
along with all the nobles and dignitaries. Everyone was so
very merry at the banquet. And throughout the land there
was such delight that the living king was giving the kingdom
to his son, for it was a great and majestic honour. What a
celebration it was, with musicians and jesters and the like.
Everything that one could wish for at a celebration was there
at this banquet.

When everyone was good and merry, the king arose and said
to his son: Since I am a seer of the stars, I foretell that one day
you will descend from the throne, so see to it that you should

not be saddened by your descent but rather remain merry. For if you will be merry, then I shall be merry, too; even if you will be sad, I shall still be merry—for you ought not be a king if you are not merry. I mean, if you are the sort of person who cannot be constantly merry, even when you descend from the throne, then you ought not be a king at all. However, if you will be happy, I shall be exceedingly happy.

The prince took to the throne quite keenly, naming the kingdom's ministers and appointing dukes and officers. The prince was wise and loved wisdom. So great sages attended him, and whenever a sage would arrive to expound some wisdom, he was treated with great dignity. He would also bestow the greatest respect and riches for the wisdom that each offered him. If one wished for money, he would be given money. If one wished for honour, he was given honour—all for wisdom. Since wisdom was so esteemed by him, everyone embraced wisdom, and the entire county was engaged in its pursuit. Since the whole country was solely occupied with wisdom in those days, they forgot about military stratagems and waging war. Even the least in this country would have been the most brilliant sage in another; the scholars of the country were sages of the most extraordinary degree.

As a result of all this erudition, the country's sages slipped into heretical thinking. The prince, too, was drawn into apostasy. For their part, the general public was not influenced by this and did not, likewise, slip into heresy. Since there was such a profundity in the sages' wisdom, everyday people were not able to delve into it and they remained unharmed by it. Only the sages and the prince became heretics.

The prince, although he was virtuous, for he was born with virtue and had fine qualities, was constantly given to reflecting: Where in the world am I? What am I doing here?, and to heaving great sighs and groans. He would consider: What does it mean for me to get caught up in such affairs? What is the matter with me? Where in the world am I?, and he would sigh deeply. Nevertheless, as soon as he began to think rationally again, he was drawn back to the study of heretical wisdom. It happened often that he would ruminate on where in the world he was and what was the matter with him, and the like, sighing and groaning. Each time he returned to his senses, he became a resolute heretic again.

And it came to pass...

A country was evacuated and all had to take flight. As they fled, they passed through a forest where two children were left behind—a boy and a girl. One family lost a son and another lost a daughter. These children were still small, around four or five years old. The children had nothing to eat, so they bawled and cried in their hunger. Then, a beggar approached them, carrying his bundles. The children began to pester him and clung to him. So he gave them bread, which they ate. He asked them, How did you get here?

They replied, We do not know, for we are only little children.

He made to leave them and they begged him to take them along. But he told them, I do not want you to come with me. Only then did they realize that the beggar was blind. They were quite astonished that he was blind, for how did he know where he was going?

It was astonishing that they were so perplexed since they were such small children. Nevertheless, they were very clever children, which is why they were so amazed.

The blind beggar gave them his blessing: May you be as I am and may you live to be as old as me. He left more bread with them and parted. The children understood that Blessed God was looking out for them and had sent the blind beggar to nourish them.

Later, their bread ran out and, again, they began bawling and crying from hunger. Then it grew dark and they finally fell asleep. In the morning, they still had nothing to eat and they bawled and cried. Just then, another beggar arrived. He was deaf and when they went to speak to him, he gestured to tell them: I hear nothing. This beggar also gave them bread to eat and made to leave them. Again they wished for him to take them with him, which he did not want. He, too, gave them his blessing: May you be as I am. Then, like the first beggar, he gave them more bread and went on his way.

Later, their bread once more was finished and they bawled and cried as before. And yet again came a beggar who was slow of speech and stammered. When they went to speak to him, his stammering was so pronounced that they did not know what he was saying. Even though he knew what they said, they could not understand him because of his stammer. This beggar also gave them bread to eat, and when he took his leave, he too gave them his blessing that they might be like him, and departed just as the previous beggars had. Thereupon another beggar arrived, and this one had a crooked neck and all transpired just as with the others. Then another beggar came, this one a hunchback. Later, yet another beggar came, with lame hands. Afterwards, there came another beggar, with lame legs. And each of them gave their bread and their blessings: that they might be like him—each and every one of the beggars in his own way.

Sometime after, the children ran out of bread again. But they had made their way to the outskirts of a settlement and found a road. They followed the road until they arrived at a village. The children entered a house where they were pitied and given bread. Then they found another house, where they were also given bread. So they started going from house to house, seeking charity. When they saw that it was all right, and they would always be given bread, they decided that they would remain together forever. They made their own large sacks so that they could go seeking alms. They attended all sorts of celebrations, circumcisions and weddings. They begged from one house to the next and went to fairs. They would sit among the other beggars at the entrances of buildings with their alms plates. After a while, the children attained renown among the beggars, who were well acquainted with the children and knew that these were the little ones who had been lost in the forest.

Once there was a great fair in a big city. All the beggars were heading there, including the children. The notion struck the beggars that the two children should become engaged and married to one another. As soon as they started discussing it, everyone was pleased with the idea. And so the two were engaged. But how could they prepare a wedding for them, they pondered. The king's name day was at hand and all the beggars would be at the celebration to cadge meat and festival loaves. From these they could make a wedding. And so it was. All the beggars came to the royal name day celebration and begged for their share of meat and bread and also collected the scraps of meat and pastry left over from the feast. Then they went and dug a deep pit that could fit a hundred people. They covered it with twigs and dirt and rubbish, and everyone assembled there. They held the wedding for the children and hoisted a canopy. And all the beggars were so very merry and the bride and groom were also very merry.

The bride and groom then began reminiscing about the mercy that Blessed God had shown them when they were in the forest. They started to weep longingly: Where can we find that first beggar, the blind man, who brought us bread in the forest?

Just as they were longing for the blind beggar, he called out, I am here. I have come to your wedding. I grant you my words as a gift that you may live to be as old as me. Once, it was but my wish for you both to live to be as old as me. But now, by the simple gift of my words I grant it: You may live to be as old as me.

Now, you may think I am a blind man, but I am not blind at all. The whole world rushes before me in the blink of an eye, a flash. (This is why he appeared to be blind, for he could not fix his gaze on the world. Not a single moment in the entire world was beheld by him, since he could not set his sight upon it.) Although I am old, he went on, I am also very young—I have barely begun to live and yet I am already very old. It is not only I who say so; I have it on the authority of the giant eagle. I shall tell you a tale, said the blind beggar.

Once some men were travelling in many ships on the sea. They were overtaken by a tempest and the ships were smashed. The men survived and they came to a tower, which they ascended. There they found all kinds of delicacies and drinks and clothes, everything that anyone could need. There was an array of good things and dainty morsels.

They decided that each man would tell a story of long ago, which he could recollect from earliest memory. Young and old were present, so the honour went to the oldest among them to be the first to tell.

The eldest then spoke: What can I say—I still remember when the apple was snipped off its branch.

No one understood what he was talking about. However, there were some sages among them, and they said: Oh, my, my! That is a tale from very long ago.

Then the honour passed to another old man, though younger than the first, to relate his memory. That man spoke: Is that an old memory?, he asked in surprise. I, too, remember that and I also recall how the candle was burning.

The sages exclaimed: Well, then this is an even more ancient memory than the first!

They were all astonished that the second man was younger and yet remembered an even older memory than the previous teller. Then the honour passed to a third elder, so that he could tell his story. The third one was younger still and he said: I recall how the fruit first began to develop, that is, when it just was becoming a fruit.

They exclaimed that this was a yet older memory.

Then the fourth elder, who was even younger, spoke: I can remember how the seed was brought to be sown to grow the fruit.

And the fifth, younger still, spoke: I even remember the wise ones who produced the seed.

The sixth one to speak, younger even than all those who had spoken before, said: I remember the fruit's flavour, before it permeated the fruit.

The seventh added: I recall the fruit's fragrance before it infused the fruit.

The eighth man spoke: I can recall the appearance of the fruit, before it had even taken shape.

I was but a child then, the blind beggar continued. I was there and this I said: I remember all that you described and yet I remember not a thing.

The sages exclaimed: This is a most ancient memory, older than all others!

They were truly astonished that a child remembered more than anyone else.

Just then, a giant eagle came and perched on the tower. He said to them: Cease your scrounging! Return to your riches and use them!

He told them that they were to leave the tower in order of age, with the eldest descending first. The giant eagle carried each from the tower. He took me first, although yet a child, since, in truth, I was the oldest of them all. He took the youngest first and he brought out the most aged elder last, since whoever was younger was indeed the older, in that the youngest could remember the earliest memory. The elder with the most years was, in fact, the youngest of them all.

The giant eagle then spoke again: I shall explain the recollections you have told. The one who recounted that he remembers when the apple was snipped from the branch meant to say that he remembers when they cut his umbilical cord at the very moment of his birth. The second, who said that he remembers how the candle was burning, was referring to the time he was in utero and a candle was above his head. That is the candle that, as our Talmudic sages of old described, illumines the head of the foetus to allow it to see in the womb's darkness. He who said he recalls how the fruit started to form meant he remembers how his body began to take shape, when the embryo was forming. And he who remembers when the seed was brought to be sown to grow the fruit remembers how the sperm was drawn to the egg. The one who remembers the wise ones who produced the seed is referring to when the sperm was still in the marrow. He who remembers the fruit's flavour means the vital lifeforce; and the fragrance is the spirit; and the appearance is the soul. As for the child who said he remembers not a thing, his memory is the utmost: he remembers what was there before the force of life, the spirit and the soul. That is why he said he does not remember a thing, for he can recall when there was nothing. He remembers everything that was happening then, and this surpasses all.

The giant eagle then told them: Go back to your ships, for they are your broken bodies and they should be rebuilt. Return to them now!, and he gave them his blessing.

Then he turned to me, the blind beggar continued, and said: You, come with me, for you are like me—as you are both very old and still young. You have hardly begun to live and you are already very old. I am like that, too.

Thus, I had it on the good authority of the giant eagle that I am both very old and yet quite young. Now I grant you these words as a simple gift, that you may be as old as I am.

And there was great celebration and rejoicing. And they were very merry.

On the second day of the seven days of the wedding feast, the bride and groom once again were given to reminiscing and this time they recalled the second beggar, who was deaf and who had sustained them and given them bread. They wept longingly, Where can we find that deaf beggar who sustained us?

Just as they were longing for him, he entered and said: I am here. He fell upon them and kissed them. And he said to them, Now I shall present you with my gift. May you be like me; may you live the good life as I have. While that is how I blessed you before, now I present you my good life by the simple gift of my words. You think me deaf, but I am not deaf. Nothing in the world is worth hearing since it is all lacking. All the sounds of the world are simply deficient. Everyone bemoans what he lacks. So even the world's joys are nothing more than imperfections, as one delights over that which had once been lacking but which one lacks no more. Nothing in this world is worth hearing that I should hear its deficiencies, because I am living the good life free of imperfection. I have it on good authority of the Land of Riches that I am living the good life.

His good life consisted of eating bread and drinking water.

He recounted:

There is a land in which the people have much treasure and live in great prosperity. Once, the rich all gathered and each one began boasting about the good life he was living. And each one described the details of his good life. Then I spoke up and told them, I am living a better life than you. So look here: if you are living such a good life, then go help out this country I know. For there is a country that once had a garden. And in the garden were fruits with every flavour and every fragrance found anywhere in the world. And in the garden could be found a dazzling array of colours, and all the world's flowers were there in the garden.

Overseeing the garden was a gardener, and the country lived the good life because of his gardening. But then the gardener went missing. Unsurprisingly, everything in the garden went to rack and ruin without a gardener to look after it and busy himself with its needs. Even so, they were still able to live off the aftergrowth of the garden.

Then there arose a new king over the country who was cruel but feckless. So he went and made a ruin of the good life they derived from the garden. It was not he himself who spoilt the garden, rather it was on account of his entrusting the country to three squads of henchmen, who he told to do as he ordered. To carry out the king's orders, they ruined the people's sense of taste. Because of what they did, whoever wished to taste something tasted only rotten flesh. And thus they spoilt the people's

197

sense of smell, so that every fragrance reeked only of turpentine. And they ruined the people's vision and made it so they saw only darkness, as if everything were beclouded.

Now, if you are living such a good life, then go help out this country. And I am telling you that if you do not help them, their ruin will be your lot as well.

The wealthy men rose and set off for that country, and I went with them, continued the beggar. On the way, each of them lived the good life of his, given that they had their treasures. As they neared the country, they, too, began to feel the spoil. First their sense of taste and then all their other senses began to sour. So I said to them, If your sense of taste, sight and smell have spoilt now, before you have even set foot in the country, how will it be once you have entered it? And moreover, how will you be able to help them?

So I took my bread and my water and I gave it to them. And in my bread and water they perceived all the flavours and smells, and everything that had been spoilt was set right.

In the land that once had a garden, the people whose senses had been spoilt began to look for a way to restore their ruined country. They recalled that the Land of Riches was nearby, and it occurred to the now gardenless countrymen that their gardener—who had gone missing and who had once provided their good life—originally hailed from the Land of Riches, where they also lived the good life. They got the notion to send word to the Land of Riches, for they would surely help them.

So that is what they did. They sent envoys to the Land of Riches. On the way, their envoys crossed paths with envoys from the Land of Riches. The envoys asked each other, Where are you going?

They replied, We are going to the Land of Riches to seek help.

The others responded, *We* are from the Land of Riches, and we are on our way to you.

Then I told them, the beggar said, You are in need of me, for you cannot go there and help them lest you suffer their fate. So stay here, and I will go with the envoys to help them.

So I went with the envoys and arrived in the county. I entered a city and saw some people coming. One of them told a joke. Then more people showed up until a crowd had formed, and they were all telling each other jokes and laughing. So I listened to what they were saying and it was all obscenities. This one told a dirty joke, then that one told one that was slightly cleaner, then another laughed and another was most entertained by it, as is common.

Then I went on to another city. There I saw two people arguing over some business deal. They went to the court to seek judgement. The court ruled that the one was owed damages and the other was obliged to pay. They left the court and recommenced their quarrelling. They said they did not want to go to the same court this time but rather a different one. So they decided on another court and brought their suit before that court. Later on, one of them started arguing with someone else, and once again they decided to take that matter to a different court. And in that way they kept on quarrelling, this one with that one, then another with someone else. Each time they chose a different court until the whole city was full of courts. The more I looked, I saw that this was because there was no truth there. Justice was being perverted for some, while favouritism distorted fairness for others. Bribery reigned and there was no truth there.

Then I saw that they were full of debauchery, so much debauchery that it was almost as if they had been granted a special exemption from basic propriety.

I told them that was why their senses of taste, smell and vision had spoilt. For the cruel king had given his three squads of henchmen free rein to go about ruining the country. They went about speaking obscenities and they brought obscenity into the country. Through obscenity their sense of taste was spoilt and everything tasted of rotten flesh.

And they introduced bribery into the country, because of which their sight was spoilt and their vision was clouded. As it is written: For bribery blindeth the eyes of the wise.

The henchmen brought debauchery into the country, because of which their sense of smell was spoilt, since debauchery spoils the sense of smell.

So, I said to them, you shall heal the country of these three sins; and you shall search for the henchmen who brought these sins into the country and banish them. And once you have cleansed the country of these three sins, I tell you, not only shall your sense of taste, sight and smell be set right, but what is more, even the gardener who has gone missing shall be found.

Thus they did. They began cleansing the country of those three sins and searching for the henchmen. They seized person after person, asking each one, Where have you come from?, until they had caught the cruel king's henchmen and banished them and had cleansed the country of those sins.

In the meantime, a commotion erupted. A madman had been wandering about saying that he was the gardener. Maybe he really was the gardener after all? Everyone thought he was mad, so they threw stones at him and drove him away. But, perhaps, he really was the gardener? So they went and fetched the man they had thought mad. I told them, He is most certainly the gardener.

As a result, I have it on the good authority of the Land of Riches that I am living the good life because I have set things right in that country. And now I grant you these words as a simple gift, the gift of my good life.

And there was great celebration and rejoicing, and they were very merry. The first beggar had gifted them long life, and the second had gifted them the good life.

On the third day the bride and groom again wept longingly: Where can we find that third beggar, the one who was slow of speech and stammered?

Just then he entered and said, I am here. He fell upon them and embraced them and said all that the previous beggars had said: Once it was but my wish that I blessed you that you might be like me. But now I grant it by my words as a simple gift: may you be as I am. You may think that I am slow of speech, but really I am not at all. It is just that utterances of this world that are not in praise of the Supreme One are worthless.

So it only seemed that he was slow of speech and unable to talk. Rather, his speech faltered in his reluctance to utter a single word that was not in praise of Blessed God—for no such speech had any value.

In truth, he continued, I am not at all slow of speech. On the contrary, I am a great orator and quite eloquent. My poems, paeans and mysterious fables are most astonishing. There is not a man alive who would not wish to hear my mellifluence, and I have that on the good authority of the greatest of men, the True Man of Mercy.

Once upon a time, all the sages were sitting together and each was boasting of his wisdom.

One boasted that he possessed the wisdom of iron; he knew how to extract it from the earth—and he brought that knowledge into the world.

And another boasted that he knew how to extract another metal—tin or lead.

Still another boasted that he possessed the wisdom of silver, and yet another boasted that he could bring forth gold.

One boasted that he could produce weapons of war.

One boasted that he could alloy iron with unusual substances.

And still others boasted of the unique wisdom that they possessed, for there are so many things in the world produced by wisdom—such as saltpetre and gunpowder and the like—and each bragged of his own particular wisdom.

One of those sitting among them declared, I am cleverer than all of you. I have the wisdom of a day.

No one understood what he was talking about.

He told them, Taken together, all your wisdoms would amount to no more than an hour. Every one of your wise ways is but an amalgam, in which individual elements have been combined. Each element has its origin on the given day that the Lord God created it. And from these minute elements come the raw materials that are wisely mixed together to create that amalgam, be it silverwork or metalware or what have you. Nevertheless, all of your wisdoms could be wisely put together and they would still amount to no more than a single hour. But, the sage boasted, I have the wisdom of a whole day.

I asked him, As which day?

He responded, Now this man here is even cleverer than I am since he asks me which day! Whatever day you wish, that is how clever I am.

Why, then, am I—the one who asked which day—the cleverest person present, cleverer even than the sage who has the wisdom of any day you wish? There is a whole story to that:

The True Man of Mercy is a very great man. And I, the beggar continued, go around gathering all true mercies to deliver to him, and these mercies are the essence of time. From the moment time itself came into being, when days and years were created by Blessed God, time has been made of mercy. Thus I go around collecting mercies to bring to the True Man of Mercy, and from those mercies time is woven.

Now there is a mountain.

On this mountain is a rock.

From this rock flows a spring.

And every thing has a heart.

The world, too, has a heart. And the heart of the world takes on the form of a whole being, complete with a face and arms and legs. And even the little toenail of this heart is heartier than any other heart.

The mountain with the spring stands on one end of the world, and the world's heart stands on the opposite end. The heart stands facing the spring. The heart keeps longing and pining for the spring, and cries out constantly in its desire to come to the spring.

The spring, likewise, longs for the heart.

The heart is doubly tormented. Firstly, it is tormented by the sun, which persistently pursues it and scorches it for longing and pining after the spring. And secondly, the heart can never cease this longing and pining, which it continues with such an intensity that it cries out constantly to be allowed to come to the spring.

When the heart needs some relief and to catch its breath a bit, a giant bird comes and spreads its wings to protect it from the sun. Then the heart can rest a little. But even while resting, it keeps its gaze fixed on the spring opposite it.

Now, if the heart longs so for the spring, why does it not simply go over to it? Were the heart to come close to the mountain upon which the spring was found, it would lose sight of the peak and would no longer be able to find the spring. And if it could not see the spring, it would die from longing—for the spring is the source of the heart's vitality. While standing opposite the mountain, the heart sees the peak where the spring is. Yet if it were to approach, the peak would be out of sight. For such is always the way with a high mountain: from a distance, you can see the peak, but up close, you can no longer see it.

If the heart cannot gaze at the spring, then it would—heaven forbid—lose its will to live. And were the heart—heaven forbid—to die, then the world would go to ruin because the heart is the source of vitality for every living thing. How could the world go on without a heart?

This is the reason the heart cannot go to the spring and remains ever standing opposite it, continually longing and crying out for the spring.

And the spring has no time; it exists outside of time. Because it transcends time, the spring has no days. But how, then, can it be in this world since nothing in the world exists without time? The only time the spring has is granted to it by the heart: a single day as a gift. Were that day to fade and disappear, the spring would be left without time, and then it would pass away from the world. If the spring were not to exist anymore, then the heart would—heaven forbid—also pass away. Thus also the world would—heaven forbid—come to naught.

So, as the end of each day draws near, the heart and the spring bid each other farewell. Then they share their poems, paeans and fables with one another—the finest fables and poetry and songs—with great love and great yearning for one another: the heart for the spring and the spring for the heart.

The True Man of Mercy oversees all this with a watchful eye. And when the day draws to its end and begins to fade away, when the spring would be left without its day and on the verge of passing away, then the True Man of Mercy comes and grants another day to the heart. And the heart bestows that day upon the spring. Then the spring has time once more.

When the day appears whence it comes, it arrives accompanied by the finest fables and songs, and in them all wisdom is contained. Each day is marked by its own distinction: for there are Sundays and Mondays and all the other days, too, as well as days marking the new moon and festivals. And whichever day comes, it arrives with its own distinct poetry.

Indeed, all the time that the True Man of Mercy has comes from me, the beggar said. For it is I who go around collecting mercies, and from them time is woven. That is why this beggar standing before you now is cleverer still than the sage who had boasted that he was as clever as any day you wish. For all time, every single day—with its poetry and fables that contain all wisdom—is brought into being by my supply of mercies.

Thus, the beggar concluded, I have it on good authority from the True Man of Mercy that I can recite paeans, poetry and mysterious fables, and all wisdom is contained in them. For all days are brought into this world on account of me. Now I grant you these words as a simple gift, that you may be as I am.

And then there was a mighty revelry with great celebration and rejoicing.

In the morning, having finished the previous day's merriment and slept the night away, they once again remembered and wept longingly for the beggar who had a crooked neck. Just as they were longing for him, he called out, I am here. Once it was my wish for you to be like me. But now, by the gift of my words, I grant it: May you be like me. You think I have a crooked neck, but I do not. In point of fact, my neck is quite straight. It is a very lovely neck. But there are worldly vanities, like a vapour, and I twist my neck so as not to loose my spirit into the world. I do have a lovely neck. A very fine neck. For I have a very fine voice. I can imitate all the world's wordless sounds with my voice because my neck and my voice are so fine. And I have this on good authority from the Republic.

For there is a Republic where everyone is learned in the art of music, in playing instruments and singing. They all apply themselves to it diligently, even the little children. There is not a child among them who cannot play some instrument or another. Even the least in the Republic would be the most excellent musical prodigy in any other country. The sages and the king and the musicians of the Republic are all extraordinarily erudite in that art.

Once the sages of the Republic were sitting down and each one was boasting of his musical skill. This one boasted of his ability to play an instrument; that one boasted of how he could play a different instrument. One boasted of his skill at yet another instrument; another boasted he could play several instruments; and another that he could play all instruments.

This one boasted he could make his voice sound like one of the instruments; that one boasted he could make his voice sound like another of the instruments. One of them boasted he could make his voice sound like several instruments; another boasted he could make his voice sound like the beat of a drum; and yet another boasted he could make his voice sound just like the boom of a cannon.

I, continued the beggar, was there as well. I spoke up and told them, My voice is better than all of your voices. So look here: If you are so wise in the ways of music, then go help out these two cities I know. For there are two cities a thousand miles apart. When night comes to those two cities no one can sleep, for as soon as night falls they all start to keen and yowl—man, woman and child alike. The very stones would melt to hear it.

Here's how it went in the two cities: If the yowling was heard in one city, then they all had to start yowling. And likewise in the other city a thousand miles away. Therefore, since you are so learned in music, help out those two cities, or at least make your voices sound like their yowls.

They asked, Will you lead us there?

I replied, Yes, I will lead you there.

They all rose and set off. When they got there and night fell, the same thing happened: everyone began to keen, and the sages joined in as well.

When they saw they could not help, I said to them, Even so, tell me, where do you reckon that yowling we hear comes from? They asked, Do you know? And I said, I do.

For there are two birds, one male and the other female, and these birds are the only such pair in the world. The female got lost, so the male searched for her, and she for him. They searched for one another for a very long time until they had both gone far astray and realized they would be unable to find each other. So they stopped and built nests. The male built his nest near one of the two cities. Not hard by, but, given the bird's voice, fairly close, since from where he built his nest one could hear his call in that city. The female built her nest similarly near the other city. And when night fell, the two birds began to keen, for he was lamenting her, and she was lamenting him. They keened with loud yowls, and those are the yowls heard in the two cities.

Because of them, everyone has to join in the keening and no one can sleep.

The sages could not believe it and said, Will you lead us to the birds?

I replied, Yes, I can lead you there. But how will you manage it? If you cannot withstand the yowling here and must all start keening, how will you make it there? You will not be able to hold out against that yowling. And during the day, one cannot withstand the joy either. For during the day, birds flock around each of them, consoling them and making them merry with their great joy, succouring them with these words of comfort: You will find one another yet! And they each of them make merry, such that by day one cannot withstand the joy. The sound of that joy cannot be heard afar off, only when nearby. But the sound of yowling one can hear at a distance, so one cannot then come near.

They asked, Can you set it right?

I answered, Yes, I can. For I can replicate all the sounds of the world. And what is more, I can throw my voice such that when I produce a sound, people nearby do not hear it, but it can be heard far away. In this way I can throw the male bird's voice to the female bird. So the call I project will reach near the place where he is, and I will also throw his voice to reach her. I will thereby reunite them.

But who could believe it? So I went and led them into a forest. There they heard:

Someone opening a door and closing it again.

And the slamming of the latch.

And the crack of a gun.

And the command to a dog to retrieve what had been shot.

And the dog floundering in the snow.

They heard it all. They looked around but saw nothing, nor did they hear a sound... And here the beggar broke off his tale and said:

Thus I have it on good authority from the Republic that I have a very fine voice and with it I can replicate all the world's sounds. And now I grant you these words as a simple gift, that you may be like me.

And there was great celebration and rejoicing.

On the fifth day, they were still merry. But they remembered the hunchbacked beggar, and they wept longingly: Where can we find that hunchbacked beggar? If only he were here we would be all merrier.

Just then he arrived and said: I am here. I have come to your wedding. And he fell upon them and hugged and kissed them. Then he said, I blessed you before with the wish that you might be like me, but now I grant it by my words as a gift: may you be as I am. I am not a hunchback at all. No, rather, these shoulders of mine are the exemplar of 'the little that holds a lot', the principle described long ago by our Talmudic Sages of old. And I have it on good authority.

Once there was a discussion where people were all boasting on that ancient topic. Everyone bragged that he had the perfect example of something little that held a lot. Each scoffed at the other boaster, as they each boasted that their own little something held a lot more than the others'. But my little that holds a lot far exceeds all of theirs.

One boasted that his brain was an example of a little that holds a lot, for his brain held myriads and multitudes of people along with all of their needs and behaviours and their experiences and actions—all of this his compact brain contains. In this way, his brain is a little that holds a lot—inasmuch as even a sliver of brain holds so many people and all that pertains to them.

But they scoffed at him, exclaiming, You are nothing and the throngs of people in that brain of yours are nothing.

Another spoke up and said, I know a little that holds a lot. Once I was passing by a mountain and I saw that it was strewn with a great deal of rubbish and filth. I was astonished, How did all this rubbish and filth end up on the mountain? A man was there and he said, It all comes from me. He had settled near the mountain and dumped there the refuse and waste from his food and drink. This was how all the rubbish and filth piled up on the mountain. Therefore, a single human being is another example of a little that holds a lot. From one person can come so much waste.

This case was deemed the same as that of the man who carried the multitudes of people in his brain.

One man boasted that he had a little that holds a lot. He had a plot of land that yielded a great amount of fruit. If someone later were to measure the fruit produced there, he would see that the total area of the plot could not possibly contain all the fruit it produced. This is, therefore, another example of a little that holds a lot.

They all were quite pleased by this fine demonstration of a little that holds a lot.

Another said that he had a very fine orchard with all kinds of fruit. Many would visit the orchard, commoners and nobles alike, for it was very lovely. In the summertime, the common folk and nobility would come for strolls there. But, in fact, there was not nearly enough space for all of these people. So this, too, is a little that holds a lot.

This pleased them all as well.

One of them said that his speech was a little that holds a lot. This man was the privy secretary of a great king. Many people came to this king, be it to heap praise upon him or ask a favour of him or the like. Of course, he said, the king cannot grant an audience to everyone, so I condense all that they say into only a few words with which I brief the king. All the praise and appeals—all that they have to say—is there in my few words. So there you have it: my speech is a little that holds a lot.

Another said that his silence was a little that holds a lot. He had been assailed by a spate of accusers and gossipmongers who denounced him and heaped abuse and slander upon him. Yet, whatever they said to defame him and whatever aspersions they cast, he kept silent. This was the solution to every difficulty he confronted and to all the calumnies uttered against him. He responded to all with his silence. So you can see that his speech-lessness is a little that holds a lot.

One said that he himself was a little that holds a lot. For there was once a poor man, and this poor man was both sightless and very large, while the fellow speaking was quite diminutive. And, yet, he guided this large, sightless poor man. Therefore, he is a little that holds a lot. After all, the sightless man could have slipped and fallen, but the small man supported and guided him. So he himself was a demonstration of a little that holds a lot, since he was such a small man who held this large sightless man.

I was there, the hunchbacked beggar continued, and I declared that this was all true, Indeed, you each have something of a little that holds a lot. I also understand the true essence of all your boasts. The least of you who has spoken—the small man who boasted of guiding the large sightless man—is, in fact, the greatest example. But I am greater still than all of you.

Now, he who boasted of guiding the large sightless one really meant that he is the force that guides the celestial circuit of the moon in its darkness. For the moon is also sightless, having no light of its own and depending on others to be visible. Even though he may be small and the celestial circuit enormous, the existence of the world is owed to him, because the world needs the moon. Therefore, he is truly an example of a little that holds a lot. But my little that holds a lot exceeds all, and here is why:

Once there was a group of scholars who were contemplating how each animal had its own preferred place for shade. Each animal has its own shaded place where it prefers to take its rest. And so, too, with the birds. Each bird has its own branch, wishing to rest only on it and not on another, while other birds choose branches of their own. The group of scholars wondered if there could be found a tree in whose shade all animals would take their rest and in whose branches all the birds would rest as well. They concluded that such a tree must exist, and they wished to go to it. The delight of this tree would be boundless; all animals would gather there along with all the birds, causing no harm to one another as they mingled and played there together. It would be a great delight to be by that tree.

So the scholars began considering how to reach the tree. A debate broke out among them that could not be settled. There was one who said that to get there one must head east, while another claimed that one must head to the west. One said this way and another said that way until they had no idea which was the right way to get to the tree.

Along came a sage who said, Why are you pondering the direction you must take to get to the tree? First you must consider this: Who are the people who may reach the tree, because not everyone can. To this tree none may come unless he possesses the qualities of the tree. The tree has three roots: one root is Faith, another is Reverence and the third root is Humility. And the trunk of the tree is Truth. Truth is the very body of the tree, from which its branches extend. Thus no one may come to the tree who does not have those qualities: Faith (by maintaining a deep belief in God), Reverence (by being God-fearing), Humility (by not holding oneself in high regard) and Truth. So the sage told the group.

But not every scholar in the group possessed all these qualities, only some. Yet there was a great sense of unity among them, and they did not want only some of them to head off to the tree while others were left behind. Thus they stuck together, even if it meant waiting for their friends as they strove towards the qualities to enable them all to come to the tree together. And so they did. They endeavoured to develop the necessary qualities of Faith, Reverence, Humility and Truth. When everyone had honed these qualities, they were of one mind and agreed on which direction to take to get to the tree. So they all set out.

They walked for a while until they saw the tree in the distance. But on closer inspection, the tree was not standing in one place, indeed it had no place at all. How could they reach it?

I was there with them and I spoke up and told them, I can bring you to the tree, even if it is not fixed in any place. For the tree transcends space, it is above and beyond any place in this world. Behold, here, my little that holds a lot. Although you have considered the little that holds a lot to be a small place that contains far more than could ever be placed in it, each still exists in space, takes up space, and is, after all, confined by space. Yet, even so, I can bring all to the tree, to a place that transcends all space. For I am the middle ground, the point between space and where space is transcended. This is my little that holds a lot: the nexus between the very edge of space and where space is no more. And I took them up and brought them to the tree.

Thus I have it on good authority that I am the exemplar of a little that holds a lot. That is why I appear to have a hunchback, because I bear so much, for I, myself, am a little that holds a lot. Now I grant you these words as a simple gift, that you may be like me.

And there was great celebration and much merriment.

On the sixth day they were merry, too, but they also spoke longingly, Where can we find that lame-handed beggar?

Just then he entered and said, I am here. I have come to you on your wedding day. He spoke to them as the other beggars had, falling upon them and embracing them: You may think that my hands are lame, but really I am not crippled at all. I do indeed have strength in my hands, but I do not use this strength in the world for I need it for something else. And I have that on good authority from the Watery Castle.

One time, several of us were sitting together and each was boasting of the strength he had in his hands. This one boasted of the particular prowess he had in his hands, and that one boasted of the particular prowess he had in his hands. One boasted he had such power and prowess in his hands he could shoot an arrow and draw it right back again. For such was his skill that even though he had loosed the arrow he could make it turn around and come back to him.

So I asked him, What kind of arrow can you draw back to you?

For there are both ten kinds of arrow and ten kinds of poison. When you wish to shoot an arrow, you daub it with one of the poisons. Doing so makes the arrow harmful. Daubing an arrow with a different poison makes each an even more harmful type of arrow. And of these ten kinds of poison, each one is more harmful than the next. That is why I asked him, Which kind of arrow is it that you can draw back to you?

I went on to ask him whether he could not only draw it back before it had hit its mark, but also whether he could draw it back even after it had hit its mark. To which he replied, Even after the arrow hits its mark I can draw it back.

But to the question: Which kind of arrow can you draw back to you?, he answered, This kind here.

I said to him, Then you cannot heal the princess. Since you can draw back to you but a single kind of arrow, you cannot heal her.

Another of them boasted his hands had such a power that whomever he took from he gave to. And as such he was a man of charity.

I asked him, What kind of alms do you give? He answered that he tithed.

So I said to him, That being the case, you cannot heal the princess either. Indeed, you cannot even get to where she is. You can enter no further than one wall of the princess's abode, but past that you cannot reach.

Another of them boasted that his hands had a particular power. He explained, There are officials in the world, each one requiring wisdom. I have such a power in my hands that by laying my hands on him I can give him wisdom.

I asked him, What kind of wisdom can you give through your hands? After all, there are ten measures of wisdom in the world.

He answered, This wisdom here.

So I said to him, You, too, cannot heal the princess. Indeed, you cannot even take her pulse. There are ten kinds of pulse and you cannot even take one, for you can give but a single kind of wisdom through your hands.

Another of them boasted that his hands had such a power that when a tempest blew he could quell the gale; he could capture the wind and restrain it and give it the moderation required of a wind.

I asked him, What kind of wind can you capture with your hands? For there are ten kinds of wind.

He answered, This wind here.

So I said to him, You cannot heal the princess. Indeed, you cannot even play the right melody for her. There are ten kinds of melody. The princess's cure is a matter of melodies, and you can play for her but a single one.

They asked me, What can you do?

I answered, I can do what you all cannot. For I possess the nine lacking aspects of each skill you boast of.

Then they asked, But who is this princess?

I replied, There is a whole story to that.

Once upon a time there was a king who was enamoured of a princess. He undertook all manner of ruse to ensnare her until he had caught her and she was his.

One time the king dreamt that the princess rose up against him and killed him. He awoke, but the dream stayed with him in his heart. He summoned all his oneiromancers and they interpreted that his dream would actually come true—she would murder him. The king had no idea what to do about her. Should he kill her? That would make him feel regret. Should he banish her? That would upset him greatly, for someone else would marry her. And, after all, had he laboured so much over her just for her to become someone else's? What is more, if he cast her out and she married another, the dream could still come true and she could kill him, since she was with someone else. But if he held on to her he feared the dream would come true. The king did not know what to do.

Meanwhile, his love gradually languished because of the dream, diminishing more and more. Her love, too, began to wither little by little until she was left with nothing but hatred for him, so she fled.

The king ordered his men to look for her. They came and told him that she was out near the Watery Castle. For there was a Watery Castle, and it had ten walls, one inside the other. And all ten walls were made of water. And the ground inside the castle upon which one walked was also made of water, as was the garden and the trees and the fruit. Everything was made of water. But the beauty of the castle and its splendour beggared description. Certainly it was extraordinary for an entire castle to be made of water. Of course you could not enter the castle because you would drown, the whole thing being made of water.

In the course of her flight, the princess reached the castle. There she was seen wandering, and that is why the king was told she was out near the Watery Castle. The king then went with his troops to capture her. When she caught sight of them she resolved to run into the castle, for she would rather drown than be captured by the king and have to stay with him. Perhaps she would escape after all and make it into the Watery Castle.

When the king spied her running into the Watery Castle he said, So be it…, then ordered her to be shot. If she is to die, let her die.

She was shot, hit by all ten kinds of arrow bedaubed with all ten kinds of poison. But the princess kept running into the Watery Castle, all the way inside. She passed through all the gates of the ten watery walls of the Watery Castle, until she had arrived deep inside the castle itself. And there she collapsed and remained unconscious. And I, continued the lame-handed beggar, am the one to heal her.

He whose hands do not possess all ten kinds of charity cannot pass through all ten walls of the Watery Castle, for he will drown.

Just so, the king and his troops pursued the princess and they all drowned. But I can pass through all ten walls of the Watery Castle.

The walls of water are the sea's billows that stand like a wall. The winds heap the waves and raise them up. And the billows that are the ten walls stand there forever; the winds hold the billows and keep them there. I can pass through all ten walls of the Watery Castle. I can draw all ten kinds of arrow from the princess. The arrows which the one boasted of being able to draw back to him come from a particular sacred verse. And the charity that is before the walls of water also comes from a verse, namely, Thy righteousness is as the waves of the sea. I can take all ten kinds of pulse through these ten fingers. For with each of my ten fingers I can take one of the particular kinds of pulse. And the ten kinds of pulse and the ten kinds of melody, these come from the Zohar, the Book of Splendour. I can heal the princess through all ten kinds.

Thus can I, indeed, heal the princess. I have such a power in my hands. Now I grant it to you as a gift.

And there was great celebration and they were very merry.

What happened on the seventh day with the lame-footed beggar—and, indeed, what became of the prince who began the tale, he never told.

And he said he never would, nor would one know it until the Messiah comes.

And may it be speedily and in our days.

Amen.

This he said:

Were I to know nothing else, it would be this extraordinary tale. For this tale is truly extraordinary. It possesses an abundance of moral edification and our entire view of the world. Contained within it are exceedingly deep mysteries, from beginning to end.

All the tales in this book plumb the world's deepest mysteries. Each word, each object, means something completely different.

And the tale
is greater
than all
else.

Translators' Note

Nachman ben Simcha (1772–1811), known more commonly as Nachman of Bratslav (though spellings of his name and city vary), was the scion of Hasidic royalty. His great-grandfather was Israel ben Eliezer (c. 1700–1760), the Baal Shem Tov, popularly regarded as the founder of Hasidism, the distinctive Jewish religious revival movement originating in what is now Western Ukraine and Poland in the mid-eighteenth century. Conscious of his pedigree and a constant seeker after religious truth, he never acquired a robust following, nor did he always seem comfortable with his own role as a spiritual leader. All in all, Nachman led an unsettled, restless life. He picked fights with, and held lifelong grudges against, the established Hasidic leadership; he went on an arduous trek to Palestine only to turn around again shortly after his arrival (and briefly to be caught up in a Napoleonic naval battle); he moved abruptly—sometimes with little warning or explanation—from town to town in and around the borderland region of Podolia (today almost entirely in Ukraine with a portion in north-eastern Moldova).

There is much conjecture concerning whatever Messianic role he envisioned for himself and his family. We know that he placed great importance on his son, whose early death marked a dramatic shift in Nachman's thought and creativity. In the wake of this tragedy, Nachman began what one biographer deemed an inward turn, plumbing his imagination for succour and inspiration.

Nachman left behind a significant volume of teachings, scrupulously documented by his close friend and amanuensis Nathan Sternhartz. What we have before us are the thirteen remarkable stories that he began to tell to his followers almost immediately after his son's death in the summer of 1806 and continued until the spring of 1810, just months prior to his own death from the tuberculosis he had contracted in 1807. While Nachman was involved in early editorial decisions in the planning stages of the book, the stories were first published posthumously by Sternhartz as *Sipurey Mayses* (*Fabulous Tales*) in 1815. Although Nachman must surely have recounted the stories in Yiddish, that volume is laid out in split pages, with the Yiddish on the bottom half and a Hebrew translation on the upper. The appearance of the Hebrew allowed *Fabulous Tales* to be viewed and respected as a holy book, rather than a secular one published in the vernacular. What's more, while Sternhartz's editorial presence is constantly felt, he is ever meticulous about indicating his own editorial interventions so that the words of the master are not in doubt. We have indicated these layers of narrative and editorial intrusion by means of typographical shifts so that Sternhartz's redactions and Nachman's pronouncements stand out, as they do to the reader of the original text.

The very same year that Nachman's *Tales* appeared in print, the book *In Praise of the Baal Shem Tov* was published, a collection of miraculous legends surrounding Nachman's great-grandfather. These were part of a popular genre of Hasidic accounts of pious and wonder-working rabbis and saintly spiritual leaders (tzaddikim). While Nachman's book appeared in that same time and context, it represents something startlingly different. Nachman's works are variously rendered as 'tales', 'stories', 'fairy tales' (*Märchen*) or 'fables', indicating a kind of intimacy that belies just how dissimilar they were to anything traditional readers had seen.

Nachman's stories are remarkably protean texts. To some they are keys to an abstruse religious-philosophical system; to others, codes to a cryptic kabbalistic or Messianic plan; to yet others, aspects of a psychological and biographical portrait; and to others still, a remarkable literary innovation. Few works of the Jewish literary imagination have such vastly different refractions. After reading, one may be baffled: what is what, then? As with the Duke of Wellington and his horse, you pays your money and you takes your choice. Our task in preparing this translation was not to privilege one or another way of reading. Instead, we want to emphasize that Nachman's stories are, crucially, all these many things, and more, at once. That is what makes them *seem* so modern or, perhaps, so timeless.

An important question when approaching Nachman's world and work is just where the ideas for these strange stories came from. One is as likely to encounter references to folklore in the scholarly search for his sources as one is to read that the tales reflect an idiosyncratic reworking of Jewish religious and mystical texts. The importance of imaginative tale-telling, however, is reinforced by influences both within and outside the traditions of Jewish culture. The rabbinic figure of Rabba bar Bar Hana, the Talmudic teller of tall tales, features extensively in some of

Nachman's earliest work. 'Fantasy' and 'the fantastic', then, are apt categories for the *Tales*.

But Jews didn't live in a vacuum, and Nachman's work is informed by far more than traditional sources alone. Among the fonts of folk and fabulous material, the *Thousand and One Nights* looms large. The work enjoyed a wide circulation in various forms both within the Middle East and beyond. Moreover, not only does Jewish material feature in what would come to be known as *The Arabian Nights*, but Jews served as important conduits for its transmission. Indeed, possibly the earliest instance of the title *Thousand and One Nights* comes from a twelfth-century Judeo-Arabic source.* Once the work made its appearance in Europe, it is likely that Jews, the majority of whom lived between Western Europe and the Ottoman lands to the East, were instrumental in mediating some of the material as it became digested into European literature. The first translation into a European language was Antoine Galland's French version (which appeared 1704–17); a German translation of some of Galland was published in 1712; and in 1718 a Yiddish adaptation appeared.† A number of Yiddish editions followed in the eighteenth century, attesting to its popularity among Jewish readers. It is no stretch to imagine a copy reaching Nachman in Podolia.

This region, whose name refers to an upland expanse of the East European Plain, had seen its share of rulers and battles

---

* S.D. Goitein, 'The Oldest Documentary Evidence for the Title *Alf Laila wa-Laila*', *Journal of the American Oriental Society* 78:4 (1958): 301–332.

† Victor Bochman, 'The Jews and "The Arabian Nights"', *Ariel* 103 (1996): 39–74; here: 44.

in the centuries before Nachman's birth. In his early years
he witnessed a dramatic political transformation that would
define the region until this very day. The shifting multiethnic,
polyglot contours of this overlapping terrain shaped Nachman's
world. Officially speaking, the Podolia Voivodeship of Lesser
Poland was where Nachman was born, in the regional capital
of Międzybóż (today, Medzhybizh), a strategic fortress town on
Podolia's northernmost frontier. Long ruled by the Kingdom
of Poland, this had been a province of the Ottoman Empire,
Eyalet-i Kamaniçe, in the previous century. As throughout the
vast area of Eastern and Southern Europe under Ottoman rule,
the Turkish presence made a significant impact on the population,
creating a distinctive culture in the Ukrainian borderlands that
were annexed by the Russian and Austrian Empires following
the partition of the Polish-Lithuanian Commonwealth in the
first years of Nachman's life.

In 1785, at the age of thirteen, Nachman married and moved
just across the Podolian border to Kiev Province, where he stayed
until his brief, fateful voyage to Palestine. His return found him
in a newly reorganized Kiev Governorate for a two-year sojourn
before he headed to what had become the post-partition Podolian
Governorate of the Russian Empire. His new home, Bratslav, was
now in that new Governorate, though it had previously been in
a separate, neighbouring Bracław Voivodeship. The erstwhile
province of his birth had in the meantime been divided between
Russia and Austria. At the end of his life he made the mysterious
decision to move to Uman—once in the Bracław Voivodeship but
now in the Kiev Governorate—to die. The geographical distances

Nachman travelled in his life were relatively small, but doing so he traversed worlds and worldviews.

Here we have fertile narrative soil of ancient and recent Jewish tradition, tilled by Lithuanian, Polish, Cossack, Russian, Austrian and Turkish boots, and watered through a thousand nights. Nachman was a product of his place, time and cultural context. Add to that the obvious parallel between the dynamic churn of his creativity and that of Scheherazade, and our title for this volume could not be avoided: *The Podolian Nights*.

Nachman's creative innovation lay in two related elements: imagination and interpretation. Once he had begun telling tales, Nachman made an about-face in his attitude towards the imagination. What was formerly shunned as conducive to evil, he now embraced as conducive to faith. The most consistent thematic through-line, no matter how attenuated it may be in some of the stories, is joyfulness, mirth and merry-making—Nachman's ubiquitous refrain. It would be easy to attribute this solely to the panentheistic Hasidic focus on a joyful interaction with life and with the world, an idea extending back to Nachman's great-grandfather. Doubtless this forms part of Nachman's interest. But it is also a way of talking about the aesthetic experience of the stories themselves, an aspect of their self-conscious literariness.

That, in and of itself, would be insufficient to account for two hundred years of rapt attention. The welter of detail and the flights of imagination have provoked immensely crafty and searching interpretations. These prove simultaneously impressive and curiously unsatisfying. The tales were originally presented orally, and Nathan Sternhartz is punctilious in his attempts to maintain their orality. The texts unspool in a way no reader could ever hope to 'decode' in the moment according to such cunning hermeneutic strategies. Rather, a story was meant to wash over us and wash away. Nachman's true innovation was the flouting of interpretability itself. All the allusions and tropes are clever clues but end up as tricksy Easter eggs (pardon the comparison). Take, for example, what should be the absolutely clear kabbalistic identification of a princess with the Shechinah, the in-dwelling of God in the world. At first glance, this is quite so; that is, until the princess goes off as a murderous cross-dressing (for lack of a better word) pirate, a-killin' and a-plunderin'. Mystical shape of the godhead indeed! Or try as you might to link the ten members of a royal retinue to each of the ten divine emanations of the Kabbalah, no one-to-one correspondence could ever be determined. Cast from the crucible of grief, these stories defy interpretation, as if at every step Nachman were challenging us: 'So you think you're so clever? Make sense of *this*!' In the words of one of Nachman's most able translators:

> The absolute symbolism forbids a rational unpeeling. When we remove the skin of the story, we find lyrical jewels. This poetic inner substance demands a nonrational, mystical response to an energy beyond verbalization. Only the poetry of modernism could teach us to experience literature on such levels.*

---

* Joachim Neugroschel, *The Great Works of Jewish Fantasy and Occult* (Woodstock, NY: The Overlook Press, 1986), 703.

How ironic it is that so much ink has been spilt on precisely such interpretive pursuits.

These *Tales* were born in translation. The first printed edition (1815), after all, contained both the original Yiddish as well as its Hebrew incarnation. But it would take almost a century before the appearance of the first translation into another language, the 1906 edition of Martin Buber. Buber was fascinated by Hasidism as a potential source for Jewish cultural revitalization. He is explicit, however, that he has not 'translated' (*übersetzt*) the tales, but rather 'retold' (*nacherzählt*) them. A variety of other English 'translators' adopted the same stance. Some translations have focused, by contrast, on the primacy of Sternhartz's *Hebrew* text in order to make a case for the place his work has in the history of that literature. While elsewhere, translations have instead taken Nachman's religious worldview as central and have included elaborate interpretational schema pegging the tales to Nachman's other writings, to Jewish sacred and ritual texts, and to Kabbalistic thought, as if the *Tales* were really nothing but sophisticated *contes à clef*, including charts and decoder guides. Our goal has been none of these. Rather, we hope to return a reading of the tales to Nachman's Podolian context, where he and his work were the product of a complicated network of social, historical, literary and cultural influences.

Buber for his part seems to be caught flat-footed by the strangeness of these stories, both in their content and in the almost exaggerated orality of their style. But instead of imputing this to a personal defect, as the historian Simon Dubnow does when he notes that 'all of Nachman's tales are the fever dream of a man sick in body and soul', Buber informs us in a headnote to his retelling of the stories that:

> the tales have come down to us in a disciple's transcript [*Schüler-niederschrift*], which has *obviously* grossly garbled and distorted the original narrative. As they currently exist for us, they are convoluted, tedious, and inelegant. I have endeavoured to preserve untouched all the elements of the original *fables*, which through their power and colourfulness demonstrated themselves to be such.*

Given Nathan Sternhartz's obsessive scrupulosity regarding Nachman's words, we know that there is, in point of fact, nothing at all garbled or distorted about the stories. Yet that is the only way Buber can account for what he regards as their convolutions, their tediousness and their inelegance. Therein lies the thorniest problem for any translator of Nachman. To some ears, these stories may not seem actually all that good, an accusation repeated by many Yiddish stylists in the twentieth century. The language is crude and unsophisticated; the editorial interpolations are excessive and often redundant; the organization can seem haphazard. In a word, they can be howlingly graceless. However, set not only within their generic congeries of sacred text, moralism, Kabbalah

---

* Nahman of Bratslav, *Die Geschichten des Rabbi Nachman*, trans. Martin Buber (Frankfurt am Main: Rütten und Loening, 1906), 1. Emphases added.

and Hasidism, but also within their Podolian ethos, they represent a literary first. Our ability to judge them for their incipient literariness is therefore inhibited insofar as on their own terms they are something new in the Jewish aesthetic world, without standards of taste and quality with which to compare them and by which to assess them. These digressive, weirdly disjointed tales may not be the honed short fiction that Eastern European letters would embrace a generation later, but, as George Saunders has observed of Nikolai Gogol, 'Since all narration is misnarration… let us misnarrate joyfully.' Nachman (and Nathan Sternhartz) would seem to agree.

The second problem is that of language. The text we have was published in two languages simultaneously, one atop the other. Blending the two would be artificial; and privileging one over the other involves a decisive choice. That the Yiddish clearly represents Nachman's original creative imaginings led us to decide to cleave to the Yiddish as our primary source and to consult the Hebrew in moments of obscurity. While not necessarily solomonic, the decision is, at least, not procrustean.

Translating Nachman, at times, could be exasperating. But, in a curious way, in the process of editing and re-editing, reading and rereading, even the most tedious stories grew increasingly compelling. While these stories bear multiple exposures, we are fully aware that few readers will undertake a rereading of them. We have therefore striven to produce a text that is simultaneously lucid in the first instance while maintaining some of the peculiarity and idiosyncrasy—if not the all-out weirdness—that hover constantly about the original.

Shortly before his death, Nachman taught, 'Faith exists only where intellect ceases; only there does man need faith. But when something is not apprehended by the mind, only the imaginative faculty remains, and it is there that faith is required.' In turning to the fanciful and phantasmagorical, Nachman shared much with contemporaries such as E.T.A. Hoffmann, Hans Christian Anderson, the Brothers Grimm, or even Mary Shelley, who warned that the vaunting scientific and technological ambitions of modernity posed grave dangers. Nachman's antidote to modernity, the balm for a world-weary Gilead barrelling towards godlessness, was storytelling. In Nachman's words: 'The world says that fabulous tales may put you to sleep, but I say that tales can wake people up.' The paradox for us is how strikingly modern those stories would turn out to be.

The Pushkin Press Classics list brings you timeless storytelling by icons of literature. These titles represent the best of fiction and non-fiction, hand-picked from around the globe – from Russia to Japan, France to the Americas – boasting fresh selections, new translations and stylishly designed covers. Featuring some of the most widely acclaimed authors from across the ages, as well as compelling contemporary writers, these are the world's best stories – to be read and read again.

MURDER IN THE AGE OF ENLIGHTENMENT
RYŪNOSUKE AKUTAGAWA

THE BEAUTIES
ANTON CHEKHOV

LAND OF SMOKE
SARA GALLARDO

THE SPECTRE OF ALEXANDER WOLF
GAITO GAZDANOV

CLOUDS OVER PARIS
FELIX HARTLAUB

THE UNHAPPINESS OF BEING A SINGLE MAN
FRANZ KAFKA